FAEBOURNE

A REGENCY ROMANCE

M PEPPER LANGLINAIS

With much thanks to Leanne, Kristen, Don, Al, and Frank for all their encouragement and perspective.

CHAPTER 1

*D*uncan Oliver was in every respect an unremarkable gentleman. He was not tall, though also not any shorter than would be deemed acceptable. He was not rich, though again not particularly in want. He was average in looks, with dark hair and clear, celadon green eyes that were easily his most striking feature. And though he rode well enough, he was not especially keen on sports or gaming. In summary, Duncan Oliver was the kind of man easily overlooked by the world. To this he had become accustomed and resigned.

And so the day someone finally did notice him became the day his life changed.

⁓

DUNCAN HAD SETTLED into one of the overstuffed armchairs of his club—a club as middling as he was—to read *Gentleman's* when George Fitzbert dropped into the chair on his left and began talking before even bothering with a greeting.

"Have you seen them yet?" George asked.

Duncan did him the courtesy of looking up from the magazine. George's caramel-colored hair trembled tenuously in its Brutus curls as George himself vibrated with all the energy Duncan never seemed to have. "Seen whom?"

"The Milne brothers." At Duncan's patently blank look, George sighed and leaned in so as to speak lower. "They've joined the club!"

Ah, Duncan deduced, *I am meant to know who these Milnes are.* "I'm afraid I don't know them," he told George.

"Of course you don't," said George. "No one does. But you should know *of* them."

Duncan shook his head. "What is there to know?"

George twisted his lips. "Little, more's the pity." Duncan knew George enjoyed gossip; not having information clearly put him out. "They never leave their estate of Faebourne. Except old Nathaniel Milne came to London some thirty years ago for a Season, found himself a bride, and disappeared again. Now his two sons are here."

"To find brides?" Duncan asked.

George shrugged and bounced back out of his chair. "Possibly. Easter and the Season are nearly upon us. Are you staying for it?" In typical fashion, he did not give Duncan opportunity to answer. "I'm off to Gully's. Care to join me?"

"You were so keen to see these Milnes!"

"And see them I will, sooner or later. But I can't sit around the club waiting. They'll turn up somewhere. Must have dozens of invitations from curious quarters."

"But they won't be at Gully's, I'll warrant." Duncan thought of the tobacco-darkened rooms and suppressed a shudder. Thomas Gulliver's home was open to comers and goers every evening, but those who wandered in and out were not of the highest quality. Duncan didn't think himself a snob, but he did have standards.

"No one knows what they're like," said George. "Being of no acquaintance, they could turn up anywhere."

"One does not find brides at Gully's," Duncan pointed out.

"One doesn't find a bride in a club, either," George said with a meaningful lift of his tawny brows. Duncan pointedly returned his attention to *Gentleman's*, and George clucked disapprovingly and made himself scarce. But George's remark left Duncan pondering what he should do for the upcoming Season. Stay in London? He was not in the market for a wife, nor would he be any mama's first pick for her daughter. Yet Duncan had stayed for past Seasons, now and then, and found them diverting at the very least.

The alternative was to go home to Dove Hill, a house as modest as was Duncan. His valet Davies would surely protest if they were to pack up and withdraw; Davies much preferred the excitement of town and did not hesitate to make his feelings known.

Well then, if only to avoid Davies' grumbling, they would remain in London for a while yet. But Duncan determined they would leave before the height of summer. The end of the Season had girls grasping for anyone within reach, and Duncan had found himself on the wrong end of their desperation once or twice. The young ladies themselves had been lovely enough and well bred, but Duncan abhorred the idea of being anyone's last resort. He would marry for love, if he ever married at all.

FROM SUCH RUMINATIONS Duncan moved on to more immediate matters, namely his dinner. Should he go back to the townhouse or stay at the club? Feeling sluggish from an afternoon ensconced in a comfy chair, Duncan felt inclined to get up and move, possibly walk home. But the thought of Mrs. Bentham's indifferent cooking gave him pause. Might he rather eat first then walk? He was standing in front of the chair, still trying to decide which way to turn, when the two men strolled in.

The taller one had closely cropped hair that was somewhere between blond and brown. And the slightly shorter one was crowned with longer, reddish-gold curls.

The fabled Milnes.

It wasn't only that Duncan had not seen them before and so assumed they were new members; the club had new members all the time, he supposed, and he could not know all of them. It was that these two young men—Duncan estimated the older one as no older than his eight and twenty—were wrapped in an aura of something unworldly. Not *other*worldly, necessarily, but something about them suggested innocence. Like a fairy tale.

Their clothing was correct and very new, very fashionable. But the way the younger one's wide eyes took in their surroundings hinted at naiveté. Duncan privately wished him away from the gaming tables. Indeed, something in him wanted to rush forward and advise them both against too much drink as well.

The young man caught him looking, blinked, and then, to Duncan's surprise, smiled and strode in his direction.

Startled, Duncan stepped backward and nearly fell back into the chair he'd only recently vacated.

As Duncan worked to keep his balance, the older Milne brother turned his attention on him. No smile from that one, Duncan noted as he looked around helplessly for someone to either call him away or intervene and engage the Milnes. But it was early yet by London's standards and the club was largely empty.

Still smiling, Young Master Milne stopped in front of where Duncan stood. Now they were closer, Duncan saw his eyes were a kaleidoscope of colors—blue and green shot through with threads of gold. The young man radiated warmth and vigor.

Not so his brother, whose eyes were a clear, cold grey that suggested granite and winter. His gaze traveled between his sibling and Duncan as though reading something in the air.

"H-hello," Duncan stammered, his usual good manners temporarily deserting him in the face of this odd pairing and their unswerving attention. "I'm Oliver. Duncan. Duncan Oliver," he clarified.

The younger one reached out and took Duncan's hand, and Duncan only stopped himself from flinching. "Thank you. I'm Edward Milne and this is my brother Richard." He pumped Duncan's hand until Duncan's arm wobbled like a gelatin.

"Let him go, Edward," Richard intoned.

Edward did as instructed but continued to smile, his eyes sparkling as merrily as a child's on Christmas morning. He glanced around. "It's very dark in here."

Duncan sought something to say. "Oh, well, clubs are usually."

Edward turned his bright, birdlike attention back to him.

"Are they? Seems a shame. We're here for dinner. Will you eat with us?"

Duncan's mouth fell open and he risked a quick glance at the foreboding Richard before answering. "That's very kind..."

"Is it?" Edward asked, and he seemed genuinely interested. "Or is it not done to ask people that?" He looked up at his brother, but Richard's expression remained, at least in Duncan's view, inscrutable. The man might have been made of stone.

After what felt like ages, Richard roused himself enough to say, "You talk too much, Edward."

Edward only smiled like it was some famous joke.

Oh dear, thought Duncan. He could not leave these two to attempt to navigate the club on their own. Duncan did not entirely understand why it mattered to him, but he felt embarrassed on their behalf. And as the first person to have formed a connection with them, he felt to some extent responsible for them, too.

Better, in fact, to remove them from the club entirely.

"I planned to go home for dinner," Duncan said. "Perhaps you would join me? It's not a long walk."

Edward's mouth fell into a little "o" like a child confronted with a much-desired treat. "Really?" He looked up at his brother. "Oh, Richard, can we?"

Richard blinked down at Duncan for a long moment before saying, "That is most kind. We happily accept."

If that is what happy looks like, Duncan thought, *I'd hate to see him unhappy*. But what he said was, "Wonderful! Well, then, shall we collect our coats?" He fleetingly considered sending an invitation 'round to George but decided not to risk it. George was likely to spread the news and show up with ten other people. As it stood, two more would set his small household to a fuss.

Coats, hats, and gloves later, they were on the streets of London. It was what Duncan thought of as the evening lull—the women were finished shopping, and the daylight was too faded to show off one's togs by promenading, yet it was too early to be out for a party or rout. The streets were mostly inhabited by darting messengers going between houses and servants out running errands and stopping to gossip along the way. It meant the three of them made an odd sight, odder even than they might have done. Edward kept gawking up at the buildings so that his steps listed this way and that, and Richard reached out regularly to redirect him without his seeming to notice.

"So," Duncan said as they walked, for Richard's silence was like a weight, "did you arrive recently in London?"

This suitably diverted Edward from his sightseeing. "Eight days ago," he said. "We've come to find—"

"Edward," his brother said, and the word was like a cut, sharp and stinging.

"Well, anyway," Edward went on without missing a beat, "we've never been, you know. To London. Where are we going?"

"My townhouse is..." Duncan felt cornered into defending himself. "It's not, you know, Grosvenor or Berkeley, but it's still a good neighborhood. Why, where are you staying?"

"Papa had a house, took us ages to find it," said Edward. "Don't know where anything is in this place. There's so much of it."

"So much of... London?" Duncan asked.

"All these buildings and roads," Edward said. "Not at all like home."

Duncan had it on his lips to ask about their home, but they had reached his townhouse, and Wilkins already had the door open. "Have two more places laid for dinner, please, Wilkins," said Duncan, trying to make it sound like having visitors was a common occurrence, and to the butler's credit, he managed to hide any surprise as he whisked away hats, coats, and gloves and then went to do as bid.

"We'll just..." said Duncan, leading his guests out of the entry and into the drawing room. It was small and somewhat sparse, though the yellow walls made it cheerful. He'd left it all the same as he'd inherited it, never having the inclination to change anything. Seeing the old chairs and scratched table now through others' eyes, however, Duncan realized it might appear shabby and outdated. At least a fire warmed the space.

But then seeing his guests' faces, Duncan wondered. For the first time Richard's flinty expression softened to something like curiosity as he gazed around at the room, and Edward had his palms pressed together, his face lit with ecstasy. "It's so..." Edward began, but then apparently lost his words.

Wilkins returned with a bow and announced dinner was ready.

"Gentlemen," said Duncan, "if you would follow me." And he led them through the double doors and across to the dining room.

Like the drawing room, the dining space was nothing special, nor was it especially large. Duncan could have fit no more than a dozen guests at table, not that he'd ever tried to fit more than half that at any given time. More often he either ate alone in the library or, when craving company, in the kitchen with Davies, Wilkins, Mrs. Bentham and Bailey.

The places for the guests had been laid to either side of the head of the table to facilitate conversation. Richard took the seat to Duncan's right, putting Edward on his left. Duncan noted the brothers' manners were correct and not at all stiff; they clearly came from quality.

"You were saying," Duncan said over the mutton, "that London is not at all like your home?"

"Do you live here all the time?" Edward asked.

Duncan shook his head. "Only when the servants get bored."

Richard cocked his head, and his grey eyes gleamed with interest. "You would not choose London over the country?"

Duncan sat back and sighed. "I don't know," he said after a minute's rumination. "I've never had to choose."

"But if you did? Have to choose, that is?" Edward asked.

Duncan considered. "Dove Hill is where I grew up. And it is roomier. I think... Yes, I would say I am more attached to it than here."

"You would choose the country," said Richard.

Duncan nodded. "Yes, I daresay I would."

Upon later reflection, it seemed to Duncan that Richard and Edward exchanged a meaningful look when he spoke those words. But retrospection is always clearer, as they say, particularly after one has been abducted.

CHAPTER 2

*D*inner passed quite pleasantly, though Duncan noticed that whenever he attempted to ask Richard and Edward about their home they redirected the conversation. Nor did they stay for port, instead pleading a need to return to their own townhouse. "We must conclude our business in town," said Richard.

"At this hour?" Duncan asked.

Edward nodded, looking for all the world like an eager pup. "Yes, we don't want to be away too long."

"But you've only just come to London," said Duncan, bewildered.

"Only because—" Edward began.

But Richard finished before his brother could say more. "We had to. It would not have been our first choice. Like you, we prefer the country."

"Oh," said Duncan, feeling oddly bereft. These two had been the most interesting thing to happen to him in a long while. At least he would have a good story to tell at the club, he being the only one to have spent any significant time in the Milnes' company. He'd surely be invited to a few more parties than usual. And George would be spitting with envy.

Richard bowed. Edward bowed. Duncan bowed. Then Wilkins bowed them out of the house and they were gone.

"Well," Duncan asked as Wilkins closed the door, "what did you make of them?"

Wilkins' lips grew tight at the corners. Duncan knew he was reluctant to tell tales; Wilkins considered himself too good a butler for that. "I could not form an opinion, sir," he said.

"I'm sure you did anyway," said Duncan with a smile, but he preferred not to make his man uncomfortable. "Well, then, I'm to bed. Send Davies up, would you?" His valet hadn't seen the visitors but would surely want to hear all about them.

Indeed, Davies lost no time coming to Duncan's chambers. "The Milne brothers, you say? Not *the* Milnes of Faebourne?"

"How does everyone know about them but me?" Duncan wondered as he passed his vest and cravat to Davies to be cared for.

Davies captured a waving arm and held it still long enough to remove a cufflink. "Ah, sir, it's an old enough story. Made fresh now the brothers have come up to London."

"So George Fitzbert said," grumbled Duncan. "Wait until I tell him they came to dinner!"

"What are they like?" Davies asked.

"Well, they're definitely different from the average. But they dress well and their manners are impeccable. The younger one—Edward—is puppyish, a bit naïve. Richard, the older one, he is more reserved. But they are nice enough fellows on the whole."

Davies pulled the nightshirt over Duncan's head. "I was more wondering whether you thought they might be fey," he said.

"I hadn't heard *that* rumor," said Duncan, cocking an eye at the valet. "You believe such things?"

Davies shrugged. "My mother did. Was superstitious, you know." He smiled and saw Duncan settled in bed. "We'll just hope you haven't angered them."

"Angered them?" Duncan asked with a frown as Davies drew the counterpane over him. "I don't think so." He thought of Richard Milne's icy grey eyes. "Would be hard to tell, but—" Edward's smile and glow returned to Duncan's mind. "No," he decided, "I didn't offend them. If anything, they were pleased."

"Let's hope you didn't please them too much, either," said Davies. He went to the door.

Duncan sat up, both tense and curious. "Why not?"

Davies smiled, but Duncan fancied it was strained. "The fairy folk are known for stealing things they like—including people."

Duncan huffed and flopped back onto his pillow. "Steal me. Really, how ridiculous."

"Good night, sir," said Davies.

"Good night," Duncan said. "Steal me," he muttered as the door closed quietly behind his valet. "I'd like to see that happen."

~

HE DIDN'T *SEE* SO MUCH AS feel it happen, at least at first. It came like a dream, the sense of movement as though his bed were swaying beneath him. Every now and then there was a bump and a jostling as though going over a stone in the road.

Road? What road? Duncan tried to roll over—that was easy enough to do in his large bed—only to come up against something padded yet immovable. Headboard? Had he turned himself around in his sleep?

Without opening his eyes, Duncan tried to navigate himself back to his proper position only to have his legs fall over the side of the bed entirely so that they dangled in open air.

"Oh!" someone said. "Richard, he's awake."

Richard?

Duncan opened his eyes.

His bedroom was not there. The swaying and jostling had, in fact, come from the coach in which he unexpectedly found himself. He had been lying on one of the padded benches and had met with the backing, only to then roll part way off the bench into a lounging slump. Discovering this, Duncan quickly sat up and found himself facing the Milne brothers on the opposite seat. Edward smiled like a happy child, but Richard watched Duncan as one might a lion at the Menagerie.

"You..." Duncan used a forefinger to draw back the curtain over the coach window on his right. It was still dark out. He let the drape drop. "You stole me?"

"Stealing is for things," said Richard. "Abduction is for people."

"Oh, well, that makes it all right then," said Duncan.

Edward's eyebrows went up. "Does it?" He looked between Duncan and Richard then laughed. "You were being funny!"

"Yes, but this isn't," Duncan said sternly. "For one thing, how did you even...?" He glanced down at himself and realized he still wore his nightclothes.

"There is a blanket," Richard said, and Duncan snatched up the woolen rectangle next to him and wrapped himself.

"This is *my* blanket!" Duncan cried, recognizing it in the dim lantern light that managed to creep in through the drapery.

"You were less likely to wake up if you stayed warm," said Edward, making it sound as though they'd done Duncan a favor.

"I was also less likely to wake up if I'd been left in my bed," Duncan pointed out.

"We regret that was not possible," said Richard.

"Not possible? Of course it—" Duncan took a deep breath and strove to sound reasonable. "Look, you clearly do not know how things work in—in London or—or the rest of the world, but you don't take people out of their houses without permission."

"Abduct them, you mean," Richard supplied.

"Right," Duncan told him. "Abducting people is wrong. It's just... It's not done in polite society." There, now. The Milnes had lived out in God-knew-where their entire lives. Perhaps they did not know any better. With a little guidance, a little instruction...

But Edward's smile vanished and his brow furrowed with concern or perplexion. "I don't think we count as polite society. Do we?" he asked looking up at his brother.

The corners of Richard's mouth tightened but he did not answer.

Indignation began to give way to a crawling fear in Duncan's chest. Gentlemen, when they saw themselves as such, adhered to a code. Admittedly, that code could be somewhat elastic (George sprang to mind), but bodily harm of another gentleman outside an affair of honor remained a firm tenet. And abduction was a definite no. But if the Milnes did not identify themselves as polite society, if they saw themselves as outside those rules...

"Perhaps if you take me home, we can figure this out in a

proper fashion," said Duncan, alarm now edging into his voice. "That is, if it's money you want, you could have chosen a better mark. But I'll do what I can for you."

"Oh, but you *can* help us!" Edward said, sitting forward and beaming again, all eager energy. "By coming with us! That's why we..." He paused to form the word carefully as though foreign to him, "Abducted you in the first place."

Duncan turned a despairing gaze to the coach window. The drapes were beginning to lighten; dawn was coming. Could he jump free? Duncan concentrated for a moment on the sway of the carriage, its rapid side-to-side motion. He would likely injure himself if he attempted to escape, nor did he particularly relish the notion of being out in only a nightshirt.

He eyed the Milnes thoughtfully. They were strange but did not strike Duncan as, say, murderers. Edward especially seemed eager to please. If they wanted to hurt him, they could have done while he was unconscious and at their mercy.

In any case, if he were facing his end, he would do so with fortitude. Squaring his shoulders, he said, "I don't suppose you packed any of my clothes." He'd also, he thought, like to meet his end in something more suitable than a nightshirt.

Edward's mouth fell open, but Richard was the one to answer. "Any need you have will be met."

"What if I need to return to London?" Duncan asked.

Neither Milne answered, and Duncan was left to peer through the tiny crack of the curtain at the grey world without while he wondered where he might be going and when, if ever, he would return home.

CHAPTER 3

"*I* warned him," Davies said, not for the first time. He, Wilkins, and Bailey sat clustered around the kitchen table while Mrs. Bentham busied herself making them tea. They were an admittedly small crew for such a large house, but Mr. Oliver needed very little and didn't, in Davies' view, think enough of his reputation to insist on a larger staff. *What must the Milnes have thought?* Davies wondered with a glance at the shaggy-haired Bailey. He was a young lad, more fit for a stable than to be serving a meal, yet his job description required him to do both.

"But why?" Mrs. Bentham asked, also not for the first time. She set steaming cups in front of each of them and the teapot in the center of the table then took her seat. "And what makes you so sure these Milnes have anything to do with it?"

"Who else?" Davies insisted.

"They *were* odd," said Wilkins.

"In what way?" asked Mrs. Bentham.

"That's just it," Wilkins told her. "I can't quite say. More of a feeling, really."

They sat for some minutes, each staring at the table or out the window, and none of them touching their tea.

"Maybe he went out," Mrs. Bentham said.

"In his nightclothes?" Davies asked. "I know every stitch in his wardrobe, and it's all present and accounted for except his nightshirt. And blanket. And slippers."

"Maybe 'e's asleep somewhere else," Bailey suggested. "Walked in 'is sleep."

Mrs. Bentham shook her head. "I went right through the house the moment we realized he wasn't in bed. He's not in any cupboard or cranny that I—"

A knock at the front door made them start where they sat, teacups rattling as they jolted the table. Wilkins sprang to his feet, immoderately energetic for one of his age. He smoothed his silver hair with his fingertips as he dashed out of the kitchen and up the stairs.

Davies, Bailey, and Mrs. Bentham exchanged glances then raced up after him. They skidded to a halt just shy of the doorway that would allow them to be seen in the front hall and gathered to listen.

"Mr. Fitzbert," Wilkins intoned.

"Hullo, Wilkins. Is he up? I heard he had quite the adventure yesterday evening!"

Davies turned wide eyes on Mrs. Bentham. Did Fitzbert know something they didn't?

The housekeeper seemed to read his mind. She gave her head a tiny shake. "If he knew anything, he wouldn't come here looking, would he?" she whispered.

"I'm afraid Mr. Oliver is indisposed," Wilkins said.

"Oh, well, I'll wait," George Fitzbert said cheerily. "Have his valet go roust him, will you?"

Wilkins cleared his throat. "That is, uh…"

Davies darted from the doorway and into the hall. "We don't know where Mr. Oliver is."

Mrs. Bentham and Bailey crept out of their hiding place to stand behind him, the housekeeper wringing her chubby, chapped hands.

"What's this adventure you mentioned?" Davies asked. "I am sorry to appear rude, but as you might guess, it's of great import to us to know anything we can."

George looked around at the lot of them. "I'm afraid I don't know much. I only heard that he left our club with the Milnes."

Davies nodded. "They dined here last night."

George's amber-colored eyes fairly popped. "Did they? What were they like? Did you hear any—?" He stopped short at the grim faces and changed direction. "Well, I mean, is it possible they'd know where he is?"

"We don't even know where they live," Mrs. Bentham said plaintively.

"That's easy enough," said George. "Gossip being what it is, *someone* knows, even if only the club. Shall I pop around and ask them?"

"I'll come with you," Davies said. At George's thunderstruck expression, he added, "In case whatever they've done with Mr. Oliver they try to do to you, too."

"Well, now, I don't think..." George began, but Wilkins, ever efficient, was already handing Davies his hat.

"I warned him," Davies said again as he strode out the door, leaving a nonplussed George Fitzbert to hurry after.

CHAPTER 4

he little bit of grey countryside visible through the crack between the curtain and the window blurred before Duncan's eyes. He could not discern where they were, had no idea how long they'd been traveling or in which direction from London they'd gone. Eventually, succumbing to the semi-hypnotic state caused by the motion of the carriage and a lack of sleep, he dozed.

The coach came to an abrupt halt, joggling Duncan awake. He blinked and squinted as the door swung open and daylight intruded. Remembering his state of undress, Duncan pulled the blanket tighter around his shoulders.

As the footman stood waiting at the open door, Edward looked between Duncan and Richard. "You will take Mr. Oliver directly up to his room," Richard instructed his brother. "We can hardly present him to Adelia in his nightclothes. Go quickly, before she realizes we've arrived."

Edward nodded and motioned Duncan toward the carriage door. For a fleeting moment Duncan wondered what would happen were he to refuse to exit. But his backside hurt, despite all the padding on the seat, and his neck and shoulders were stiff from having slept at an inopportune angle. It felt good to move, however awkward the situation.

And it *was* awkward. Wrapped in the blanket and trying to

cover as much of himself as he could with it, Duncan ducked toward the daylight then paused at the sight framed by the carriage door.

Grey stone stretched to either side as far as Duncan could see; he had to turn and lean out of the coach to find the ends of the house. It was gloriously carved, practically gothic, with an ornate crest above the door featuring a creature Duncan could not name—something like a fox crossed with an eagle and maybe a bit of lion. High above, along the roofline Duncan spied figures whose graceful forms suggested angels. The place might as easily have been a church as an estate.

However, though most estates familiar to him sat in wide, green spaces, this one did not. The trees encroached upon the sides of the house, wild and untrimmed. They were, Duncan noted, very leafy for so early in spring, and the grass equally green. Flowers, too, in a riot of colors dusted the lawn in front of the house. There seemed no reason to them, no pattern, no plan as to their placement. Duncan wondered whether the Milnes were in want of a gardener.

A nudge at his back returned Duncan to himself and he stepped carefully down from the coach to the short gravel path that led to the steps up to the house. He was grateful his abductors had at least thought to bring his slippers, though the mental image of them wedging his footwear onto his feet while he slept was simultaneously amusing and disconcerting. Duncan supposed he should be just as glad they *hadn't* attempted to fully dress him.

All at once, Edward had his arm and was leading him forward. "Welcome to Faebourne," he said, all but panting with enthusiasm. "It will be such fun! But first—" Duncan nearly tripped up the few steps to the house as Edward propelled him. "We must get you dressed."

"You should have taken my valet when you took me," Duncan remarked dryly.

The humor was lost on Edward, whose kaleidoscope eyes widened a trifle. "We never thought of that."

The entry hall passed in a blur. Duncan had the impression of highly polished floors and an impossibly high ceiling as he was drawn up the curling staircase. At the first floor, Edward diverted to the right and directed Duncan down a long hall to a room at the far end. There, Edward threw open the door to the largest bedroom Duncan had ever seen; it seemed to him one could keep three, perhaps four, coaches in it, horses and all.

As things stood, however, only furniture inhabited in the room: a large four-poster that could sleep half a dozen with space for each to roll over, a Camelot-sized round table with two high-backed chairs in front of a fireplace large enough for a child to stand upright in, and a smaller desk against the wall beside a wardrobe so tall Edward could have stood on Duncan's shoulders and still his head would not have come level with the top of it.

"Were you expecting a giant?" Duncan wondered aloud as Edward urged him forward into the room.

"Not this time," Edward replied, "though one never knows around here."

Duncan opened his mouth to pursue the topic but Edward continued to push him toward the wardrobe. "Everything you need is there." He hesitated and began twisting his fingers into complicated shapes. "I am sorry we didn't think to bring your valet..."

Duncan stepped to the wardrobe and opened one of the two cathedral-sized doors. Clothes hung inside, and there were drawers beneath. As for the shelves above, Duncan thought he would need a ladder to reach them.

"Hats," said Edward.

Duncan looked at him questioningly.

"Up there. Hats," Edward explained.

Duncan nodded and withdrew a shirt. It appeared to be the correct size for him. "How...?"

"Faebourne always knows," said Edward. His fingers began to twist again, and he stepped from foot to foot. "Do you need someone to...?"

"What? Oh, no. I'm sure I can manage," Duncan said. The idea of a stranger helping him dress when already he felt himself to be in a vulnerable position made him uneasy. He would contrive to do it himself during his unexpected holiday. "I don't expect I'll be here long?" he asked.

Edward bit his lip. "Well!" he said abruptly. "I'll leave you to..." He waved at the wardrobe. "And then come fetch you for some breakfast." When Duncan glanced at the bright sunlight streaming in through the window, Edward amended, "A late breakfast. Well, late for us. London..." He shook his head. "It's very different there."

"Yes, well, there's no place quite like London," Duncan agreed.

Edward nodded eagerly and backed out of the room, closing the door as he left.

Duncan waited a moment then went to the one tall window in the room to look down and judge his chances of escape. What with all the curlicues and jutting bits of masonry, he thought it possible to climb out and down. Then what? He looked at the trees beyond the small apron of lawn behind the house. They grew close and thick, a veritable forest.

He would go around the front, then, down the drive or whatever this place had. He would find the road and walk until a carriage came by or he happened upon another dwelling. Until help could be secured.

But he could not do all that in his nightshirt.

Reluctant as Duncan was to make use of his hosts' bizarre hospitality, he saw no other option. From the wardrobe he withdrew a green-gold vest and bottle green jacket to add to the shirt he'd previously extracted. He found pantaloons, stockings, smallclothes, and finally a neckcloth that he tied in a very simple style while wishing Davies were there to do it for him.

In the corner of the room on the far side of the fireplace, Duncan discovered a tall—everything in the room was tall—looking glass that allowed him to admire his work. Not bad, he decided, even with the modest knot in his cravat. He only needed shoes.

He was peering under the bed in search of appropriate footwear when the door opened once more and Richard entered. Duncan rose from the Lotto carpet to find Richard's grey eyes surveying him sternly. "I just, erm..." Duncan said and held out a foot.

Richard's eyebrows rose in comprehension. "You haven't any. Yet."

"I beg your pardon?" Duncan asked. "I can hardly go down to breakfast in my stockings!"

"No one here will take offense, I assure you," Richard told him. "Just do be careful of Aloysius; he sometimes nibbles toes." With that, he turned on his heel and marched out of the room, leaving Duncan no recourse but to follow or starve. Shoeless either way.

CHAPTER 5

*T*hus Duncan Oliver found himself padding in stocking feet after Richard Milne, down the long corridor and the twisting stair, trying all the while to keep from slipping and adding to his indignity.

As they came around the final curve of the staircase, Duncan glanced up from where he'd been watching his feet and discovered Edward waiting in the entrance hall. Beside him stood a petite but slender young lady with hair so pale as to be almost white. She wore a blush-colored dress and held a ginger cat in her arms. No, Duncan amended upon another look, it was a small dog. Or no, upon further scrutiny he deduced it was a fox.

The lady smiled as Richard and Duncan approached, and Duncan noted a repressed energy in her akin to Edward's, a mixture of enthusiasm and innocence and wonder. Her eyes were widely set and cornflower blue. "At last!" she cried.

"I am sorry if I've kept you from your breakfast," Duncan told her with a small bow.

She startled him by placing a hand on his arm. "Not at all! I am only so glad you've finally come! This is Aloysius," she added, promoting the fox with her other arm. "He's happy to see you, too."

The fox appraised Duncan with its golden eyes and, remembering Richard's warning, Duncan instinctively curled his toes.

"This is Adelia," Edward announced somewhat belatedly. "Our sister."

Duncan bowed again. "Miss Milne. Pleased to make your acquaintance."

The lady giggled, not in the loud, false, cringe-inducing way of some ladies Duncan had known, but in the light and wholly comfortable way of someone truly pleased and amused. "And you, of course, are Mr. Oliver. Edward has told me all about you."

Considering Edward hardly knew him, Duncan wondered what the young man could possibly have said either for or against him. 'He is easy to abduct,' perhaps? Did that count as for or against?

The fox shifted in Adelia's hold, and she bent to set him down. "Yes, all right, go on," she said in the tone of a mother allowing a child to toddle off, and the animal pranced away across the entry with great poise.

Adelia watched her pet go, laughed again, and took Duncan's arm. "You must be hungry."

"Oh," Duncan said. "Er, yes, I suppose I am." *And my feet are cold*, he thought, but he kept that to himself.

Adelia steered him toward the dining room, her brothers trailing behind them. The room, like everything else Duncan had thus far witnessed at Faebourne, seemed unnaturally large, even for such a sprawling estate. It was painted in cool lilac hues and had tall windows all along one side that Duncan suspected could also be used as doorways to the pillared porch beyond. The dining room draperies were sage green with cream and gold trim. The table itself could easily have seated some two-dozen guests, perhaps more. Its dark surface gleamed with polish, and Duncan felt almost sorry to have to mar it with his touch.

Adelia marched him to the far end of the table and, so quick and silent Duncan had not realized he was there, Richard came to stand on his left. Duncan scuttled sideways, but that only put him closer to Miss Milne, and it took him a moment to understand they expected him to sit at the head of the table.

They don't understand how this works, Duncan thought. But should he try to educate them or simply follow along with their odd ways? Which would get him home faster? Or at the very least get him shoes?

"Oh, well, I—" he began uncertainly, but at Richard's cold and level stare, Duncan dropped into the chair with no further protest.

The rest of the party arranged themselves with Miss Milne to Duncan's right, Richard on his left, and Edward on his sister's other side. Duncan sat and waited, unsure what to do. There had been no platters on the sideboard when they entered, no redolence of food. His stomach gave a soft growl even as he considered all possible scenarios.

And then as though from thin air a footman appeared at Duncan's elbow to set a heaping plate before him. Eggs, ham, and toast with jam crowded the china.

"I hope it is to your liking," Adelia said.

"It looks and smells delicious," Duncan told her as he waited for the others to be served. A second footman came around with tea for the gentlemen and hot chocolate for Adelia.

Glancing around again, Duncan thought, despite the house's façade and the Milnes' seeming lack of society, Faebourne did not appear to be a place stuck in time. No one wore archaic clothes and the furnishings were not relics. In fact, for such a forbidding, gothic exterior, the interior of Faebourne was quite comfortable and inviting.

Well, aside from forcing guests there against their wills. If only they'd extended a proper invitation, Duncan would have been well pleased with the situation.

He'd just picked up his fork when a far less agreeable thought occurred. *Might they poison people?* He wondered how he'd let his guard down so quickly. Davies would certainly have scolded him to be more cautious.

"You're not eating," said Edward.

Duncan forced a smile. "Apologies. I was wool gathering."

"Sheep?" Edward asked.

"What?" Duncan returned. "No, I... I don't know why they call it that, actually..." Duncan felt in danger of losing his thread of thought. "I mean I was thinking." His eyes fell again to his untouched food, and his stomach gurgled more insistently this time. He didn't much like his chances if he starved himself. He'd be too weak to escape or get very far if he didn't keep his strength up. Poison would be a faster way to go, though probably no more dignified.

Refusing to allow any more doubts to seep in, Duncan put a resolute forkful of eggs into his mouth.

Around the table, Duncan sensed his hosts relax a trifle. Or had that been his imagination? He waited for the adverse effects. Nothing happened.

Unless they'd used something slow? In which case, not wanting to linger in pain, Duncan ate faster.

"So," said Duncan after several more mouthfuls of breakfast, "this is Faebourne? I've heard of it, of course, but—"

Richard interrupted. "Heard of it? Where? From whom?"

Adelia leaned forward in her seat. "What did they say about it?"

Duncan's gaze bounced between them, but for politeness finally settled on Miss Milne. "When your brothers came to London, they joined my club," he explained. "And your family name preceded them."

Edward's brow furrowed. "What do you mean?"

"Well, I'll admit I hadn't heard of you myself," said Duncan, feeling the need to tread carefully. They seemed nice enough people, if eccentric, but they'd thought nothing of abducting him for whatever reason. "But my friend George mentioned Faebourne. It's old, isn't it?" George hadn't said as much, but it felt like a safe assumption given the architecture. And better, he thought, to stick to discussions of the estate rather than conjecture about the reclusive family.

But Richard would not be sidetracked. "George who?"

And Edward asked, "Do we know a George?"

"We don't know anybody," Adelia told him gently. "Not even a George."

Duncan wondered if being on the front line of a battle felt like this—the confrontation, the pressure from all sides, and no chance for retreat. At least the Milnes hadn't brought muskets to the meal. Still, evasive maneuvers were called for.

"Fitzbert," Duncan said, answering Richard. "He was only excited because, as I said, he knew of Faebourne."

"But he's never been here," said Edward wonderingly. "No one ever comes here. Except you."

Duncan was tempted to point out he hadn't 'come' to Faebourne so much as been forcibly escorted but decided it an unnecessary contention. Best to simply go with things as they flowed. Instead Duncan asked, "Well, do you ever invite anyone?"

Three pairs of eyes blinked at him.

"Perhaps that is why no one ever comes?" Duncan suggested in a small voice.

Adelia smiled. "You are correct, of course. You see, we have no acquaintance. We are far from anyone here and..." She gave a tiny shrug.

"There must be a town or village?" Duncan insisted. "Where does your cook buy supplies?"

The Milnes exchanged a flurry of glances that made it seem as though this had never occurred to them.

"Or you could go to London," Duncan continued, warming with hope. "I would be happy to introduce you to my friends."

Edward beamed at this, and for a moment Duncan believed he'd succeeded in gaining approval for his idea. But then he saw Miss Milne hang her head, and Richard scowl, and Edward's smile faded like sun behind a cloud.

A needle-like pain in Duncan's left big toe caused him to yelp and kick out involuntarily. His actions did not in the least appear to unsettle his hosts, however; both men remained seated, and Adelia ducked under the table in a most unladylike way, crying, "Aloysius! No!" She emerged with the fox in her arms, and Duncan could swear the little beast was grinning at him.

"Richard, you should have warned him," Adelia said.

"I did," Richard replied with no apparent aggravation over the matter.

Duncan wanted to argue that if he'd only been given shoes there would not have been any problem, but he restrained from criticizing his hosts. Ideally his sojourn at Faebourne would be short. The Milnes were only lonely for company other than their own and their servants'. The novelty of having a guest would wear off eventually.

Or, if more guests came, perhaps they would no longer find him so entertaining. "If you cannot go to London, perhaps it could come to you," he suggested. "That is, if you'd like to meet George, or any number of other people, I could easily arrange it."

Edward smiled broadly again, and Duncan felt his heart lift with optimism. But then Edward said, "We met the person we wanted to meet. We met you."

Duncan stared at the young man for a long moment then at Richard, whose face appeared impassive as ever. Finally he turned to where Adelia sat, still cradling her pet fox in her arms. She smiled, though it wavered.

"I sent them, you see," she said. "I sent them to fetch you to Faebourne."

CHAPTER 6

"It's just as well you're dressed fashionably," George grumbled as he and Davies left the club. "Where did you get those togs, anyhow?"

"Mr. Oliver and I are of a size," said Davies. "He allows me to keep his castoffs. One should be ashamed to have a poorly dressed valet in any case."

George surreptitiously considered the man who walked beside him down the street. Not only of a size with Duncan, but of an age, too, by George's estimation. Similarly dark hair, but while Duncan's eyes were green, Davies' were sable. "How did you come to be his valet?"

Davies' brows lowered and those inky eyes narrowed. "What makes you ask?"

George shrugged. "Only curious. If I'm going to be seen with you all over town, I'd like to know something of you."

Davies straightened his shoulders, but all he said was, "What was the address again?"

George briefly considered pursuing his curiosity but decided to let it lie for the time being. "St. James's, if you can believe it," he said. "Seems the house has been in the family a long time."

It was not a long walk given the club was on Pall Mall. George could sense Davies' desire to rush ahead, but George set a sedate pace. No reason to appear frantic in public, and Duncan was unlikely to be in any real trouble. Nothing interesting ever happened to Duncan. George liked him for that very reason; he felt fascinating by comparison.

They turned the corner to St. James's Square and found the correct address, one of the many imposing structures that faced the Square. George knocked at the door, and they waited. And waited. And continued to wait, their heads tilted toward the door as they strained to hear any sound from within.

They were just beginning to look apprehensively at one another when a maidservant passed by and said, "Begging your pardon, sirs, but they've gone."

"Gone?" George asked. "But they'd only just arrived!"

"Do you know where they went?" Davies asked. "Did they have anyone with them?"

Confronted with such terse questions, the maid began to shift from foot to foot, eying the two men warily. "Home, I suppose. They left dreadful early. I only know because..." She blushed.

"It doesn't matter how you know," Davies said, not unkindly, and the maid gave a tremulous smile. "But if you could tell us what you *do* know, we'd be most grateful."

The maid nodded. "It was just them, the two gentlemen. Odd enough, that. No servants or anything. Did all for themselves, the horses and whatnot." She made a gesture that indicated the stables in the mews behind the building. "Well, an' a driver appeared once they'd hitched up. Dunno what they must've been in a hurry not to have the driver or a stable lad do the work. No luggage, neither, that I saw."

"And they left early this morning?" George asked.

The maid nodded again. "Can't help but notice two gentlemen doing up their horses and carriage at that hour. Hour of the Fairy Folk, my ma would have called it." She peeked up at them from under her lashes and blushed again. "Silly, I know."

"Maybe not," said Davies, and the maid's eyes went wide at his grim tone.

"What?" she asked. "Has something happened? Had to skip town, did they?" She looked up at the townhouse, her face creased with disappointment. "They seemed harmless enough. The younger one smiled at everyone who passed."

"No reason to be alarmed," said George brusquely. "We're only looking for a friend that we thought might be visiting here. Clearly," he spread his hands, "he is not. Come along, Davies." He stepped down the stairs and past the maid.

Davies paused long enough to fish a shilling from his waist-coat pocket and press it into the maid's hand. "Thank you again," he said, receiving ever more blushes in return.

"Davies!" George's voice echoed back to them.

The valet tipped his hat to the maid and followed.

"Now where are we going?" Davies asked as he caught up.

"Only one place to go," said George. "Faebourne."

Davies would have stopped walking if he hadn't needed to keep pace with George. "Faebourne? But no one's ever been. I'm not sure anyone knows where it is."

"It exists," George said. "Somewhere. I'm familiar with someone who would know about the land grant it would have required. Historian," George sniffed then sighed. "Useful bloke, though. Has won me more than one wager."

Davies tried to assemble this information in his mind. "And how do you know this historian?" From the tales Duncan told, it seemed unlikely that George Fitzbert and historians haunted the same places.

George's mouth grew tight. "He's my brother. Not," George added swiftly with a sharp glance in Davies' direction, "that he does anything so low as *working*. No. Henry just... *enjoys* it for some reason."

"You make it sound like a sin," Davies remarked.

"It is, of a sort. A sin against pleasure rather than one prompted by it." George sniffed again. "He is almost certainly ensconced in the reading room. If anyone can find the information we need, Henry can."

In two more turns, they were standing before a somewhat grimy window behind which shadows of people moved between desks set like islands throughout the room. George turned to Davies and held a finger to his lips then gently pushed open a door so well oiled it let out nary a creak.

Upon clearer view, Davies saw that the desks were long and had many people seated at them a fair distance apart so that none would disturb another. Each of these people had a book—or several—in front of them, while still other visitors strolled along the walls, which were lined with tall shelves. The air was dry and smelled of something pleasant, though Davies could not guess or even describe the scent.

George stopped just inside the door, leaving Davies to catch and ease it closed. The muffled quiet of the place made Davies almost afraid to breathe. George turned this way and that, tails of his coat flying. Then, seeming to have spotted what he sought, he started resolutely across the room with Davies hurrying after.

They came to a halt beside one of the desks, where a man sat bent over an open tome. Beside the book lay a drawing that Davies soon realized was a map. The man scarce seemed to notice them; George softly cleared his throat, and only then did the gentleman look up. With a lurch of surprise, Davies observed a more than passing resemblance between the seated man and the one standing beside him. The same caramel-colored hair, if not as consciously styled, and the same amber eyes. He opened his mouth, would have involuntarily exclaimed at the sight, but George cut him short by holding up a hand.

"Yes," he hissed quietly, "we are twins.

"Henry," George continued in as low a voice he could manage and still be heard, "we have need of your expertise."

Henry glanced around then nodded and stood, closing the book he'd been reading. "I must re-shelve this," he said. He rolled up the map and held it out to his brother. "Take this for me and meet me outside."

George stared at the proffered map as though it might be a snake, so that Davies was moved to take it instead. When Henry raised an eyebrow, George affected a hasty introduction. "Henry, may I present Davies. Davies, my brother Henry."

Davies gave a slight bow.

"Just Davies?" Henry inquired.

George's mouth fell open. "Well, he... he is only a... an acquaintance."

"Owain," Davies supplied with another small bow.

Henry's face split with a broad smile. "Like the knight?"

Davies grimaced. "My mother was fond of fairy tales."

Henry appeared prepared to pursue the discussion, but George said, "We wouldn't want to disturb the other..." He glanced around. "Readers. We'll meet you outside, Henry."

Davies felt he had no choice but to follow George out.

"IT'S RATHER A BRILLIANT IDEA," Davies mused as he and George waited. "Books for anyone to come read."

"We have books enough at home," George grumbled. "I can't imagine why Henry would waste his time here."

Just then the door opened and Henry stepped out. In the sunlight, Davies was struck anew with their similarities: a slightly more than average height and sturdy build with broad shoulders, even down to the buff pantaloons and shining brown boots. Only the colors of their coats—George's being claret, Henry's a more sober Prussian blue—and George's more careful coif hinted at the differences in personality that lay beneath the nearly identical surfaces.

"So," Henry said, "Owain, is it? And your mother fancied fairy tales? Well, but Arthur is more of a roman—"

"Where is Faebourne?" George asked flatly.

Henry drew back slightly from the abrupt question, his gaze darting between his brother and Davies. "Speaking of fairy tales," Henry said. "Though of course it exists. You know," he went on, pinning his attention to Davies, "in some stories, Owain is the son of Morgan le Fey." Davies only smiled wanly and handed Henry the rolled map, which he accepted with a resigned sigh. "What do you want with Faebourne?"

"The Milnes have—" Davies began, but George broke in.

"The Milnes have invited us, but alas, they forgot to give us the direction, and they've already left town."

"That's odd," said Henry.

"*They're* odd," George insisted. "Or haven't you heard?"

"How did you meet them?" Henry asked.

"At our club," said George. "Now, will you help us or won't you?"

"It's in Kent," said Henry. "I don't know exactly where, but with a little research—"

"How quickly can you find out?" Davies asked.

Henry's brows rose again at Davies' suppliant tone. "By this evening, if you allow me to..." He pointed at the door behind him.

George gave a sharp nod. "Good man, Henry. Shall we meet you here?"

"We can hardly talk inside," said Henry, "and I'd rather not hold court on the pavement. Why not meet at home?"

George rolled his eyes and turned to Davies. "If he isn't here, he's at home."

"It wouldn't kill you to be home once in a while either," said Henry. "Mama says she'd have forgotten what you look like if you didn't look exactly like me."

"Very well," said George with a grimace. "We'll see you at dinner. It seems," he added to Davies as Henry returned to his books, "you are to meet my mother."

CHAPTER 7

"*S*-sent for me?" Duncan stammered.

Edward nodded eagerly, and Adelia nuzzled Aloysius as though to draw comfort from her pet. "Yes," she said softly. "Isn't that right, Aloysius?"

"For me?" Duncan asked again. "Specifically?"

"Well..." Edward began.

"Not by name," Richard said, and in the large room his voice seemed to boom like thunder.

"Let's go into the Small Room," Adelia said, "so that the dishes can clear." Duncan supposed she meant so the staff could clear the table, though he'd yet to spy any such staff aside from the silent footmen. Well, not everyone befriended their servants the way he had. If anything, he was an outlier.

Adelia set Aloysius down and he pranced to the dining room doors then paused and waited for them to rise and follow.

We are following a fox, Duncan thought. It felt important somehow to narrate events in his mind; doing so kept him sane and grounded. Otherwise the circumstances became too unreal, and he began to question whether these things were really happening.

Aloysius walked in stately fashion, leading them to the front of the house and, indeed, a small room situated there. The windows let in the morning light, giving view of the riot of colorful flowers he'd noticed at arrival. The walls of the room were dove grey, the drapes duck-egg blue, and the whole of the space soothed his soul.

Adelia settled into a dainty armchair and gestured Duncan onto the settee while Richard and Edward took their seats on the larger sofa opposite. Aloysius sat at his mistress' feet, head lifted to watch Duncan. Self-consciously, Duncan slid his stockinged feet away from the fox and drew himself farther back against the somewhat overpadded furniture.

Smoothing her skirts, Adelia turned to Duncan and said, "It is only the three of us, you see, now that Papa is gone."

Aloysius whined softly and looked back at her. She patted him. "Yes, you're right, there are four of us."

"Adelia..." Richard said, his voice low, almost a growl.

"We should tell him," she said. "How else is he to...?" Her attention returned to Duncan, and he felt her gaze as a physical thing, a warmth that crawled up his spine. The way the morning light touched her face made her seem to glow. "Or maybe," she said with a slight frown, "we should first ask what you know of Faebourne?"

Edward sat forward like a child anticipating a great story, his multicolored eyes alight. Richard only straightened his shoulders, his face creased with discontent. *Or perhaps*, Duncan thought, *worry?*

Duncan shifted where he sat, all too aware of the attention. "If you wanted someone who knew the story of your home and family, you chose poorly. I am apparently the only man in London—when I was in London, that is—not to have heard of you. George—"

Edward clapped his hands with delight. "*Who* is this George you continue to speak of?"

"Edward," said Richard quashingly.

Duncan's thread of thought frayed at the interruption. "A friend of mine. He's, you know, the type to have all the tattle."

"Tattle?" Adelia asked.

"Gossip. Information," Duncan clarified. "Though London gossip isn't always true. One must guard against..." He waved his hands in search of the word. "Falsehoods. Sometimes the stories start out true, or merely as speculation, and then... grow."

The three Milnes and their fox stared at him for a moment before Adelia said, "Please, Mr. Oliver, do go on."

Duncan cleared his throat. "There isn't much to go on about. All I'd heard was that your father appeared in London some thirty years ago, found a bride, and disappeared again. And so the—the supposition was that you..." He put his hands out, palms up, to indicate Richard and Edward, "had come to London to also find brides. But as you've abducted me, rather than... Well, I can only assume the rumors were mistaken."

He paused and attempted to read their expressions, but Richard's was like granite, Edward appeared only entranced, and Adelia had the studious expression of one being taught a complex lesson. Aloysius, on the other hand, seemed to smile.

Finally, Adelia spoke. "My brothers are not in need of wives, at least not yet." She threw them a small, fond smile. "I, on the other hand—"

Something dreadful twisted in Duncan's stomach as comprehension struck him. The Milne brothers had not sought brides for themselves but a groom for their sister! Dear God. To be ensconced with this family, isolated in the middle of who-knew-where, for the remainder of his days? Never seeing his friends, or Dove Hill... And what would become of Wilkins, Davies, Mrs. Bentham and Bailey? Duncan could not tolerate the thought. He shot to his feet and took a few stumbling steps backward. Never mind shoes, he'd go in his stockings. "I really... I can't—" He turned and dashed out of the room, slid across the entry, and made for the hefty front door.

Behind him, Aloysius let out a bark, and Duncan tensed himself for another attack from the little ginger beast, but it failed to come. Nor did he hear any cries or shouts from the Milnes. For a fleeting instant, Duncan thought perhaps they would let him go.

He wrenched open door and half jumped, half fell down the brief flight of steps. Once on the ground, the gravel of the front walk immediately began to tear at Duncan's feet, shredding the thin stockings and slowing him considerably.

Still, he might have escaped if not for the trees.

Unlike the sides of the house, which were crowded with trees, the front of Faebourne had only a few smaller shrubs close to the building before relinquishing ground to the overgrown carpet of grass and flowers. The short front walk cut through this lawn before opening to a circle for carriages. Some few feet to the right and left of the carriage drive stood a line of what Duncan could only assume were very old trees given their size. Ash, he later thought, or oak, his knowledge of trees not being terribly extensive.

Duncan reached the carriage circle and turned blindly to his right, straying onto the grass to spare his feet, his only goal at that moment being to get away, though at the same time he marveled that no one had come after him. He heard Aloysius howl; it sounded like a call of some kind. And out of nowhere— Duncan would have avowed it had not been there before—a tree root rose up and tripped him.

Not to be thwarted by such, Duncan managed to keep his balance and keep going, only to have a low-hanging branch catch his hair. It took a little longer to free himself of that obstacle; he had in fact done so, when he met another tall root and low branch at once. *Surely that is not natural*, Duncan thought, even as he bounced off them and landed on his arse in the grass. When he looked up at the offending tree, nothing about it appeared out of place. No lifted root, no drooping branch. Yet he heard a low, persistent creaking, like that of old wooden floors walked on or doors opened after years of disuse.

Duncan turned to look over his shoulder. No roots, no branches that fit the description of the assault he'd just been subject to. Yet one of the trees appeared to be straightening, as though it had bent over to pick something up and now meant to stand tall once more.

Slowly, warily, Duncan got to his feet. Something rustled above him. A bird? A squirrel? He peered up but could not see anything moving in the branches.

"Oh! Are you all right?" Adelia appeared at the mouth of the drive, Aloysius beside her.

"That fox is laughing at me," Duncan said as they hurried over to where he stood.

Adelia did not deny it, instead saying, "Your poor stockings! And your feet! You must come back inside."

But Duncan did not budge. "Why am I here, Miss Milne?"

She pressed her palms together and looked up with a plea in her face. "Please, Mr. Oliver. I—" She glanced down at her pet. "*We* will tell you everything if you'll only come back."

Duncan glanced up again at the tree. "It hardly seems I can leave."

Adelia smiled, but Duncan fancied there were tears in her eyes. "Faebourne is... strange."

"Am I prisoner here, Miss Milne?"

She hesitated a bit too long for Duncan's liking before shaking her head.

"I have your word on that?" he asked.

Another pause before she nodded.

"When will I be allowed to return to London?"

Duncan watched the delicate bob of her throat as she swallowed. "Please," she said again. "If—if you prove unmoved by our story... You will be free to go."

At her feet, Aloysius whined, and she looked down at him, blinking. "We cannot keep him against his will," she said.

Duncan sighed. "This would have gone much more smoothly if you'd only extended a proper invitation," he said. "As it is..." He scanned the trees again. "It is highly irregular. And somewhat unfriendly," he added.

Adelia bent down and scooped up the fox. "Oh no," she said, "no, we don't mean to be inhospitable, not at all! Do we, Aloysius? But some things..." For a moment she appeared frightened, but she took a deep breath and rallied. "Some things must be done a certain way."

"Tradition?" Duncan asked.

Adelia's expression became one of determination. "Ritual," she said.

CHAPTER 8

*A*fter a day of assuring Wilkins, Bailey, and Mrs. Bentham that he and George Fitzbert were doing all they could to locate Mr. Oliver, Davies finally set out for the Fitzbert residence in Hanover Square. He'd borrowed Duncan's evening clothes, as he'd never had reason to keep any himself, even when Duncan handed them down. Davies lived vicariously through his employer, and much of his amusement depended on his ability to convince Duncan to go out or, even better, have guests himself.

And so a mixture of excitement and nerves swirled within Davies as he was bowed into the highly polished entry of the townhouse. For once, he was the one out in society. It was the life he might have had, if—

"Ah, Davies!" George exclaimed as the butler showed Davies to the drawing room. George made unsteady progress toward where Davies hovered on the threshold, and Davies realized that George was already well into his cups. This understanding must have shown on his face, for George leaned in—Davies tensed, ready to steady him should he topple—and said, "Takes courage, you know, to dine with Mummy.

"You look natty," George went on. "More castoff togs, eh? You wear them better than Duncan, I daresay. Brandy?"

"No, thank you," said Davies.

George shrugged and made his indirect way to the tray on

the table. On it sat the decanter and three glasses. "Brought it from the library," he muttered. "No proper sideboard in here, you know."

Davies *didn't* know, but did not bother to say as much. He inched into the room, which he found to be comfortable if somewhat feminine. The creams and yellows and ruffles and whorls gave the impression of being inside an oversized pastry.

"Sit," George instructed, gesturing with his glass in a way that alarmed Davies, if only because it might spill and stain the furniture. To avert calamity, Davies swiftly moved to take a seat on the striped satin sofa lest George have cause to gesture again. He had hardly settled himself, however, when a stately, grey-haired woman wearing a deep shade of lilac entered the drawing room, and he was forced to spring to his feet again.

"Ah, Mother," said George. "May I present my new, er, acquaintance? Davies, this is my mother, Mrs. Frances Fitzbert."

Mrs. Fitzbert frowned at her son, and Davies winced inwardly. It was not strictly an incorrect introduction but might have been handled with better grace. If George felt his mother's displeasure or his guest's discomfort, though, he failed to show it. He merely knocked back the remainder of his drink.

"That's quite enough, George," Mrs. Fitzbert said. She turned to Davies with a speculative gleam in her cognac-colored eyes. "Davies?" she asked, and her tone was a sharp crack that cut through the room. "No relation to Lady Georgiana Lyming, are you? She married a Davies, I believe."

Davies bowed in acknowledgement. "She was my mother."

"What?" George asked. "You're a lord?"

"No," Davies said flatly, hoping his tone scotched further discussion.

But Mrs. Fitzbert pursued the subject. "Lady Georgiana married beneath her. Family disowned her, as I recall."

"You recall correctly," said Davies.

"Oh ho!" said George. "Scandal! I had no idea. Dinner may be more entertaining than I thought."

Davies pressed his lips together and did his best to keep his expression neutral. *This is why I cannot go out in society. Why didn't I simply lie?*

"She clearly taught you to do the pretty in any case," Mrs. Fitzbert said. "George, you could take some lessons from this one." She turned back to Davies. "I wonder how the two of you became acquainted?"

"Friend of Duncan Oliver," George said, and Davies let out a private sigh of relief at not being introduced as a valet, even if it was the truth.

"Duncan is such a good boy," said Mrs. Fitzbert with the first hint of warmth to her tone that Davies had heretofore witnessed. "I only wish you'd be more like him, George."

"Or like me?" asked a voice from the parlour doorway as Henry appeared.

"I'm enough like you," said George. "Brandy?"

"Later," said Henry congenially. "We should go in to dinner in any case." He held out an arm for his mother to take, but Mrs. Fitzbert ignored it.

"Dodson hasn't announced dinner," she said. "And in any case, I shall go in with Mr. Davies. His mother was daughter of an earl. It really is too bad," she added to Davies. "She and I had our come out at the same time, and I remember how lovely she looked at every ball and party. We all envied her, of course. Beautiful *and* wealthy? Hardly seemed fair." She sighed. "What a waste."

Davies ground his back teeth together to keep from responding. He wished he'd accepted the brandy after all.

Almost worse than Mrs. Fitzbert's words was the odd mixture of sympathy and curiosity in Henry's eyes. "Davies?" he asked. "I don't recall an earl—"

"Of course not," Mrs. Fitzbert snapped. "Davies was her married name. Nothing special about *him*. A fair nobody as it were."

"Might I remind you, Mother," said George, "that you have no title either? You are a Missus and we are simple Misters. Fair nobodies are we, in no position to pass judgement. But apparently in every position to be rude to our guest."

Mrs. Fitzbert frowned around at her son. "Rude? It's not as though Mr. Davies doesn't know his own history." She peered—not quite up, as she was not much shorter—at Davies and asked,

"Not tetchy about it, are you? No, didn't think so. There, you see, George. He's not offended."

Just then the butler, who Davies assumed to be Dodson, appeared in the doorway. "Dinner," he intoned with bow lower than strictly called for.

Mrs. Fitzbert latched herself to Davies' arm. "What did your father do again? Soldier or something, wasn't he?"

"Naval captain, ma'am."

"Away often, was he?"

"Yes, ma'am."

"Can't have left you much."

Davies did not answer.

"My late husband didn't amount to much either," Mrs. Fitzbert said as they entered the dining room. "We're better off without him. Sit here, on my right," she instructed. As they sat, she went on, "Lived off my dowry, but thank goodness I had the sense to make some investments before he spent it all.

"Was she happy?" Mrs. Fitzbert asked abruptly.

Davies looked up sharply from the empty plate he'd been contemplating. "I'm sorry?"

"Your mother. Was she happy?"

Davies had the sudden urge to laugh and cry at the same time at the recollection of his mother's gentle smile. Somehow, he got the words out. "Yes, ma'am. She was the happiest person I have ever known."

"Beautiful *and* happy," murmured Mrs. Fitzbert as footmen set the soup in front of them. "Hardly seems fair."

TO DAVIES' relief, the conversation then turned away from his family and background. Henry took it upon himself to extemporize on facts about Kent. "Used to be a kingdom in its own right. Very green, lots of orchards and such," Henry told them. "And Canterbury, of course."

"An orchard in Canterbury?" Mrs. Fitzbert asked absently as she dipped a spoon into her orange cream.

"No, I meant— Well, I suppose there might be... I could look it up for you," Henry offered.

"We'll establish the truth while we're there," said George.

His statement snared his mother's attention. "There? Where? Kent?"

"Oh, so you *were* paying attention," George said. "Yes, we're planning a trip to Kent, which is why Henry so graciously read up on it."

Mrs. Fitzbert reared back her head to examine Davies next to her. "Storming the castle walls, are you?"

Davies had begun to appreciate the reasons George avoided meals at home. He wondered whether George bore the brunt of Mrs. Fitzbert's attention when there was no guest present to divert her. "Pardon?" he asked now.

"That's your mother's part of the country," Mrs. Fitzbert told him. "Off to hit up the old family and see if they'll accept you?" But when she saw Davies' bewildered expression, she relented. "Seems not. You didn't know?"

Not trusting himself to speak, Davies only shook his head.

Mrs. Fitzbert clucked. "Have to wonder if she ever told them about you then."

George slammed his palms to the table, startling everyone. "I thought you had a function this evening, Mother."

Mrs. Fitzbert blinked at her son. "What? Oh, yes. Lady Darley is hosting a musicale."

"You hate musicales," said Henry.

"One doesn't say no to the Darleys," said Mrs. Fitzbert. She rose and the gentlemen started to as well, but she waved a hand and sailed for the double doors. "No need for that. Do at least let me know before you dash off to Kent, George."

"You'll hardly know I'm gone," George said.

"I hardly know when you're here," his mother agreed. "Still, I prefer to be informed of your exploits before rather than after. Good evening." She disappeared in a puff and rustle of lilac.

George, Henry, and Davies waited, looking at one another as the sound of Mrs. Fitzbert's steps faded from the entry hall.

"Well," said Henry after a moment, "let me show you the map."

CHAPTER 9

*D*uncan limped up the front steps after Adelia, his pride as injured as his feet. He'd failed utterly to escape, and now they would be watching him all the more closely. Not that he planned to try again in any hurry. Blast those trees. What the devil had happened?

Adelia led him back to the Small Room where Edward stood at the window (surely, Duncan thought, he'd seen the entire debacle) and Richard remained ensconced on the sofa. Like a chastised schoolboy, Duncan returned to his place on the settee.

"We will need to salve his feet," Adelia said, setting Aloysius down, and the fox promptly pranced off to who-knew-where.

To Duncan's horror, Adelia then knelt in front of him and reached for his left ankle. Instinctively, he drew it away. She blinked up at him. "I only meant to remove your stockings."

"I—" Duncan began, thinking this was something better tended to by himself in private, but it seemed unlikely they would allow him any discretion after his recent escapade. "I'll do it," he finished. He peeled off what remained of the ruined hosiery, all too aware of the attention being paid to him and his now bare feet. Across from him, Richard continued to stare. And though Edward was positioned behind him, Duncan could sense the young man's excitement; the very air in the room vibrated with it.

Adelia made a sympathetic sound, bringing Duncan's attention back to his hurt. "You are bleeding," she said.

Duncan turned a foot for a better look at the lacerated sole. "Not much. Should probably stay off the rug, however."

Aloysius returned then bearing the handle of a small wicker basket in his mouth. He brought it to Adelia and sat down beside her, turning his molten gaze on Duncan. From the basket, Adelia extracted a small pot of ointment, a tea towel, and new stockings. Had the fox somehow...? *No*, Duncan thought, *impossible*. More likely a maid gave the beast the basket to carry. Except how would the maid know what was needed? And why not bring it herself?

So tangled was Duncan in this winding thread of thought that he was startled when a cool hand took hold of his foot—so startled that he very nearly kicked Adelia in the face. "What are you doing?" he demanded.

"The salve," she said, holding firm to his foot with one hand and dipping two dainty fingers into the liniment with the other.

Duncan twitched in her grip. "It's really not... *done*, you know. For a lady to..."

Adelia paused and frowned up at him, though she did not let go. "For a lady to what?"

"Would you rather Richard or I do it?" Edward asked, rounding the settee and thus coming back into Duncan's view. "Neither of us are ladies."

"That's not really the..." began Duncan, but he was at a loss for words when it came to explaining the proprieties. Where even to start? He sighed. "No. Thank you. I can balm my own feet."

"But I already have some on my fingers," Adelia said. "I might as well—" And with no further hesitation, she swiped the ointment onto the bottom of Duncan's foot.

Duncan's foot jerked, and Adelia asked, "Did that hurt?"

"No," Duncan answered through gritted teeth, and this time he managed to successfully pull free. "It tickles." He reached down and scooped up the pot to finish the job.

Upon closer inspection, his feet were hardly battle worn. Despite the few punctures and scratches and little bit of blood from the gravel, his soles were dirty and tender more than damaged. And in the spot where Adelia had placed the cream, Duncan's foot had grown warm and slightly numb.

"What is this?" he asked, inspecting the nondescript pot. No label. He sniffed at it. The ointment had a light fragrance that Duncan could not identify.

"We make it here," Adelia told him. "It is mostly chamomile, yarrow, and patchouli. Why?" she asked. "Is it not working?"

"On the contrary, it works almost too well," said Duncan. "I can no longer feel my feet."

"Oh, it always does that," said Edward. He folded himself to squeeze in beside Duncan on the settee and leaned forward to inspect Duncan's freshly daubed soles. "You might not want to try walking for a while. Not until the tingling stops."

Adelia picked up a stocking and showed every sign of being about to slip it onto one of Duncan's feet. He snatched it from her fingers. "As I'm immobile for the time being, why don't you tell me the reason for my being here?" he suggested as he urged the sock over his slippery foot.

Duncan saw the glances fly from one Milne to another, including the pet fox. A silent conversation seemed to occur in the air around him. Duncan waited, but none of them appeared willing to speak. So he chose to prompt them further.

"You said something about a ritual?" He tried to keep his tone light in an attempt to disguise his growing unease. Rituals were for church: christenings, weddings, holidays, funerals and the like. He had no interest in participating in any such thing, particularly without knowing his role.

Adelia made a delicate sound in the back of her throat and—reluctantly, Duncan thought—met his gaze. She looked like a supplicant, kneeling there at his feet, and he wished she would get up and sit in a proper chair. But she stayed put as she spoke, one hand reaching blindly to stroke Aloysius as she explained.

"You thought perhaps that my brothers had gone to London to fetch me a husband," she said. "If only it were that simple."

Duncan released a breath. He would not be forced to marry Adelia Milne. The relief buoyed his heart despite her visible solemnity. Whatever worried her, whatever reason she and her brothers had for bringing him to Faebourne, it could not be so terrible. "Well, then," he asked, "what seems to be the trouble?"

"My—our—mother believed I was not her child," said Adelia.

It took Duncan a moment to reason that out. How could a woman give birth to a child and not believe it was her own? Davies' mention of fairy folk sprang to mind and then he understood. "She thought you were a changeling?" Duncan asked. At Adelia's sober nod, he said, "I've heard of women taken by a fever after childbirth... They are not themselves. You should not allow it to distress you."

Adelia smiled in a way so genuine and frank that Duncan's heart rose a little higher on the tide of his good feeling. If this was Miss Milne's chief concern, it would be easily vanquished, and he could go home that very afternoon.

"I would not be distressed if Mother had not..." She glanced across at Richard, whose frown was like granite, his grey eyes like flint. "If she hadn't acted upon her fears," Adelia finished, her voice warbling slightly over the words.

Something like fire ignited in Duncan's chest, a fury at the idea this lovely young lady might have been abused. But one look at Richard told Duncan this was unlikely. The eldest Milne would not have stood for it, Duncan was certain. Still, he felt compelled to ask. "Acted upon it in what way?"

Adelia bowed her head, and it was Edward who answered. "Mum cursed her."

The pretty blonde head sank lower, and Duncan turned to the young man beside him. "Come again?"

"Cursed her," Edward repeated. "And of course Mum made it impossible for *us* to break the curse, so..."

Oh dear. They are *touched.* If the story of their mother was true, lunacy likely ran in the bloodlines. Still, his odds were better if he played the hand as dealt. "So you need me to break this curse?" Perhaps he could playact his way through whatever ritual they'd made up and come off none the worse.

Adelia nodded, and Duncan spied the movement of her throat as she swallowed. "We should not have waited so long, but I hesitated until the last possible moment to let my brothers go to London. I was so worried for them!" She turned her wide eyes on Duncan in a plea for understanding. "I thought, somehow..." Her shoulders slumped, and her voice became so low Duncan almost couldn't make out the words. "Somehow we would find a way around it."

"But you did not," Duncan surmised. "And your brothers went to London to find a—a champion for you?"

"It must be done before Adelia's twentieth birthday," Richard said. "Which is a fortnight from today."

A fortnight! Would they keep him a full two weeks? Hopefully, whatever his task, he could complete it well before then, and once done he would be free to go.

"Well," said Duncan more cheerily than he honestly felt, "whatever it is, I'm sure we..." He glanced around at his hosts' somber countenances. "Or, erm, *I* can manage it in a timely fashion."

Adelia's head snapped up, her wide eyes shining. "Then you will stay and help us?"

"Well, I..." Did he have a choice? Adelia had told him that they would let him go if, after he heard their story, he did not want to stay. But her big blue eyes, the grin on Edward's face, and the... somewhat softening? expression on Richard's usually stony visage made Duncan feel appreciated—needed—and gave him purpose for the first time in ages. He was self-aware enough to know he was no hero, but to these eccentric Milnes he might become one. He could not imagine they would ask him to do anything dangerous.

"I can try," said Duncan. "Though I cannot promise I'll be successful. I'm hardly a knight in shining armor."

Adelia clapped her hands. "Splendid! Then first we must make your shoes."

"M-make them?" Duncan asked.

Around him, everyone rose to their feet, including the fox. Edward startled Duncan by taking his arm and helping him to his feet. "Think you can walk now?"

"Oh, I—I think so," said Duncan. "But did she say *make* shoes?"

"It isn't shining armor you need," Richard said, "but grass slippers."

CHAPTER 10

"*A* rather generous grant of land," said Henry. He, George, and Davies stood around the library table where Henry had laid out a map of Kent. He inscribed a large, irregular circle on an unmarked region of the chart with his forefinger. "The house could be anywhere in this area. I couldn't find an exact location. Seems the estate is mostly forested."

"There's a road at least," said George. "There must be."

Henry shrugged. "Not on record, not that I could discover. Doesn't mean there isn't one, of course, just means I can't give you better directions. Sorry," he said. "I did my best."

"Thank you," Davies said as George opened his mouth to respond in what Davies felt sure would not be gratitude. "It's more than we knew before."

Henry smiled at Davies then looked to his brother. "How is it you have such well-mannered friends, George, when you yourself are such an ill-tempered reprobate?"

"At least I have friends," said George. "All you have are books and—" He waved a dismissive hand at the map on the table.

"Thank you again," Davies put in firmly, sparing a glare for George, "for using your extensive learning to our benefit."

"Yes, well, it's nice to have a purpose in life," said Henry. "Something to occupy one's time. Hobbies."

"I occupy myself quite well," George said. "My hobbies are clothes, drink, and gaming."

"As long as you don't bring home any unwanted brats," murmured Henry. He rolled the map and handed it to Davies. "Do take care of it. Else it'll be on my head if I can't return it in good order." He made as if to go then turned back. "When do you expect to leave?"

Davies looked to George, who seemed suddenly to have found something interesting in his fingernail. With no help from that quarter, Davies answered, "I don't know. As soon as we may, I think."

Henry nodded, made it two steps farther then turned again and cleared his throat. "What Mother said, you know..."

Davies held up his hands almost as though to stave off a blow. "Please, you needn't—"

But Henry pressed on. "I was only going to say, the Montcliffe seat isn't far from the Milne estate."

"Montcliffe?" Davies asked.

"Lord Montcliffe," said Henry, and when Davies' expression remained blank, "Arthur Lyming, Earl of Montcliffe. Lady Georgiana, that is, your mother, was his daughter."

Davies only stared.

"I am sorry," said Henry with a slight bow. "I did not mean to interfere." And this time he succeeded in exiting the room.

Davies turned to George, who continued to examine his hands. "You didn't know," George said as he used a thumbnail to push back a cuticle.

"No," said Davies. His mother had never spoken about her family; Davies had only learned she was a lady because everyone else addressed her as such. "Lyming," was the only name she'd ever mentioned and, having absorbed his mother's injured feelings toward her kin, Davies had never pursued the connection.

George nodded. "Henry is insufferable when it comes to these things. Peerages and whatnot." He sniffed and finally looked up. "What's the use of knowing about all these families if you're only going to hide in a library and read? Might as well go and meet some of them. They're out and about, after all; you can knock into any one of them on any given afternoon." George eyed Davies speculatively. "You're probably the first new person Henry's met in at least a year. You and your fairy tale name and your romantic past..." He snorted. "Catnip to Henry. To him, you're like something out of a book. He doesn't mean any harm, mind. Seems he got the brains and I got the charm."

'Charming' was not the first word Davies would have used to describe George Fitzbert, but he could appreciate the attempt being made to assuage his feelings. "How *did* you and Mr. Oliver meet?" he asked.

"He never told you?" When Davies shook his head, George smiled. "He's not one for stories, is he? Pretty dull, actually. But sometimes dull is a good thing."

George's oddly wistful expression made Davies' stomach clinch, though he couldn't have said why. So instead he remarked, "Mr. Oliver does prefer the quiet life at Dove Hill. He only stays in London to keep the staff happy. We get bored, you know, isolated like that."

"I haven't had the pleasure of Dove Hill," said George, his mouth puckering sourly.

"Mr. Oliver probably suspects *you* would be bored, too."

George's gaze traveled upward to the ornately moulded ceilings. "Would be nice to get away from here sometimes, though."

"Are you here year round?" Davies asked.

"Yes," George said. "This is it, you see. Our 'estate' as it were. We haven't some grand manse elsewhere. Just... this.

"Well," George went on with new gusto, "it seems my wish is to be granted in any case. We will set off first thing tomorrow morning. I'll fetch you in the curricle as it's on the way. You'd best go and pack. It won't take a day to get there, but may take some time to find the place, so plan for an indefinite journey. Though I suppose you can wash your own clothes, eh? Ha!"

Davies frowned, not at the slight but at the forced nature of it. There had been no true mirth behind the comment; rather, it evinced subconscious habit, as though George were used to tossing off cutting remarks. Davies suspected George had said it as a way of distancing himself from any genuine feeling.

Then again, Davies decided, he couldn't and wouldn't presume. The day's excursions aside, his familiarity with George

Fitzbert came mostly second hand via Duncan's summaries of their doings, and knowing Duncan, he likely left off the worst of it to keep his friend from appearing bawdy.

Straightening his shoulders, Davies said, "So long as you don't expect me to wash yours," and turned to go.

"Fair enough," said George. "Be ready at first light. Would be bad form to keep your employer waiting for rescue."

Davies paused at the library threshold but did not look back. "Mr. Oliver would surely consider himself to be at fault for having left without notice." And with that, he went in search of Dobson to fetch his borrowed coat and hat, George's whip-crack of laughter echoing behind him.

CHAPTER 11

$\mathcal{D}$uncan was certain he had misheard. "*Grass* slippers?" he asked as he followed Richard Milne out of the room.

They made a strange procession: Adelia and Aloysius in the lead, followed by Richard, Duncan, and finally Edward. Adelia led them down the entry hall, past the dining room, and to the back of the house to a door as heavy with ancient timber as the front one. Yet despite its size and apparent weight, Adelia pulled it open with no visible effort.

They stepped one by one out onto the colonnaded portico Duncan had noticed through the dining room windows. The gothic stonework was mottled by age, and the whole of the design reminded Duncan of a cloister, if only there had been a courtyard. But this veranda gave way to a green apron of lawn before being set upon by the cluster of trees.

Adelia took the small step down to the grass, and Edward— or perhaps Aloysius; Duncan was not sure—yelped in alarm while Richard said warningly, "Adelia..."

She turned and smiled, though Duncan saw apprehension in her eyes. "I'll only go this far. See? It's all right." She stopped and surveyed the too-long grass around her. "How much do you think we'll need?"

Edward dropped down and put his face very close to

Duncan's stocking feet. "He's feet are long but rather narrow." Edward sprang back to standing. "More than for me, but less than for Richard, I'd guess."

Adelia nodded and sighed. "Well, best to work then."

Richard and Edward promptly joined their sister on the lawn while Duncan lingered on the step, not quite ready to submit his feet to more abuse, though the grass appeared soft enough. Beside him, Aloysius sat with his tail curled around his paws, head lifted to scrutinize him.

"What?" Duncan asked him. *Zounds, they have me doing it, and I haven't even been here a day.* Whatever abnormality ran in the family, he hoped it wasn't catching.

"Try to find long ones," Adelia instructed. "They will be easier to weave."

Her voice recalled Duncan to the odd activity and the notion that he would finally be given shoes... of a sort. With a regretful grimace at his fresh stockings, he stepped out onto the grass. It *was* soft, and warm from the overhead sun, though it wouldn't be long before the trees' shadows crept out of the forest and cooled things.

Adelia turned her smile on him as he approached, and this time no apprehension marred her visage. In the sunlight her hair appeared silvery, and her eyes mirrored the blue of the sky. Her pale skin fairly glowed. "You will damage you skin if you do not fetch a bonnet," Duncan told her.

"Adelia never bothers with things like bonnets or gloves," said Edward as he gently tugged blades of grass free and laid them on the growing pile beside him.

"She shouldn't be outside," Richard intoned. Duncan observed that the elder Milne struggled to pull up grass without breaking the fragile leaves; his discards heaped nearly as high as those collected.

"Why shouldn't you be outside?" Duncan asked Adelia. "You came out earlier, when I..." Yet he found himself oddly reluctant to bring up his escape attempt, nor did he particularly want to talk about the trees. At the thought of them, he looked askance at the forest standing not two yards away.

Adelia's gaze followed his. "As long as I stay within certain distance of the house—"

"An *un*certain distance," said Richard. He snorted in disgust at another ruined tendril and tossed it aside.

Edward sat back to appreciate his mound of grass. "Adelia turns into a beast if she gets too far from Faebourne."

"An enfield, technically," Richard said. "Like on the family arms."

Duncan recalled the crest on the front of the house and the oddly amalgamated creature featured on it. He glanced between the two men and then at Adelia beside him. Surely they were having him on. But the seriousness of their faces said otherwise. Even Aloysius appeared grim.

Well, and was it any stranger than anything else they'd said or done?

Actually... yes, Duncan decided. To say your sister turns into a heraldic beast was even stranger than making grass slippers. Stranger, too, than whatever had happened with the trees. After all, Duncan could pretend that had been a figment of his imagination. He could tell himself he'd only stumbled over some roots and run into a low-hanging branch. And so, for want of a way to similarly discount the Milnes' claim, he asked a most childish question: "How do you know?"

The very sunlight seemed to slip away from Adelia's face, to be replaced by a shadow of sorrow. She turned toward the trees.

"Adelia, no," said Richard. He threw down the grass he held and started to stand, but his size made him slow. Edward, meanwhile, watched open-mouthed as his sister took one, two, three tiny steps away from the house. She held her right arm outstretched in front of her, her posture one of reluctance, like someone who has been dared to hold a hand over a candle flame.

Duncan watched, fascinated. Here was the moment of truth. Either magic inhabited Faebourne or some kind of inherited insanity did, though Duncan supposed the two were not mutually exclusive. Perhaps magic made one insane?

Adelia gave a sharp cry and her outstretched hand trembled. For a fleeting second Duncan thought he saw feathers beginning to form over the back of it, the fingers themselves appearing to harden, curve, and sharpen. But it ended in an instant when Richard pulled Adelia back a few paces.

Adelia pulled her hand in to her chest as though to cradle something injured. Duncan began to ask whether she was all right, but Richard overrode him, telling his sister, "You have nothing to prove to this—" He glared at Duncan. "Person," he finished, spitting the word as though it tasted bitter. Duncan suspected Richard would have liked to use some other words but was too gentlemanly to do so in the presence of a lady.

"He is here to help us," Adelia said. She looked at the piles of grass. "But first we must help him. That should be enough. Let us bring it into the kitchen."

Edward dutifully scooped up the accumulated turf and headed into the house. Richard lingered until Adelia gestured for him to go. With another hard look at Duncan, he followed his brother.

"I am sorry," Duncan said once he and Adelia were alone. Well, alone under Aloysius' watchful gaze. Did a fox count as a chaperone? "I didn't mean for you to..." To what? He didn't know what he'd meant or not meant to happen. "To get hurt," he finished weakly.

"I can't fault you for being skeptical. It is, as I understand it, rather out of the ordinary."

"That's putting it mildly," murmured Duncan as they stepped into the shade of the veranda.

"I wouldn't know, of course," said Adelia. "To me it is quite normal. This is the only life I've ever known."

Duncan glanced at the young woman beside him, and her downcast eyes and forlorn expression fractured something inside his chest. He might not be a hero, but the least he could do was try to break Miss Milne free of whatever held her. Spell, curse, figment of her imagination—whichever, he would do his best to free her of its grip.

"I hope," he said, and when she lifted her face to look at him, the words stuck in his throat. With a small cough he started again. "I hope perhaps I'll have the pleasure of broadening the scope of your, er... experience." He paused. It hadn't come out as gallantly as he'd planned. In fact, it sounded almost like an improper overture.

"That's not..." Duncan began, meaning to correct himself, but Adelia smiled.

"I would like that very much," she said, then surprised him by taking him by the arm. "We will work in the kitchen because the trees cannot see us from there."

As she led him inside, Aloysius at their heels, Duncan wondered if winning Adelia Milne her freedom would cost him his.

CHAPTER 12

"*H*e's here," said Davies. He and the rest of the household had been gathered by the front window all morning in anticipation. At the arrival of George's curricle, Davies took up his rather shabby portmanteau, succumbed to a kiss on the cheek from Mrs. Bentham, nodded to Wilkins and Bailey, and went to meet his traveling companion.

The sky over London was pearly grey with coming dawn, leaving anyone awake to question whether it would remain so all day or turn to blue. As Davies wedged his bag next to George's much larger trunk on the board behind the seat, he wondered whether they might be sorry for the lack of cover, as the curricle had none. If it rained, they'd be wet, and if it shone, they'd catch the sun.

George appeared to have no such qualms. Indeed, he was indecently spirited for the early hour, smiling and chatting. He told Davies all about the matched greys that pulled the curricle (Thunder and Storm) and went on to talk about what Davies could only imagine was every other horse George had ever come into contact with.

"I'm being led to believe," Davies finally broke in, "that you delight in horses."

George laughed, and Davies marveled at how much more carefree he seemed as they left London behind them. "We can't keep many, you know, living in town as we do," George said. "And Duncan—Oliver, that is— "

"He refers to you by your Christian name as well," said Davies. "I do believe he considers you his closest friend."

George fell silent for a moment. "Well, I still have not been invited to Dove Hill, so we cannot be *that* close."

"Mr. Oliver does not invite anyone to Dove Hill," Davies told him. "It's small, for one thing, and Mr. Oliver has done nothing to renovate it since his parents passed some years ago, meaning it is somewhat outmoded. Nor is he fond of hunting or any of the usual ways of passing the time in the country. He fears guests would be bored. Lord knows we are." This last was said under Davies' breath, but George heard it all the same.

"Who?" he asked. "The servants?"

"Mr. Oliver is happy to read all day and take walks when the weather permits. But Porterdale—that is the town nearest Dove Hill—has little to offer by way of amusements. Or gossip. Or anything to divert us, really."

They lapsed into quiet, and Davies noticed the buildings becoming further apart as the road rolled on. He supposed they were fortunate it hadn't rained recently, as surely the wheels of the curricle would founder in mud. "A curricle isn't usually used for longer trips, is it?" he asked.

"Mother would hardly let me have the chaise. Anyway, this allows us to travel in style."

"It has no head," said Davies with a squint at the still-grey sky. He hoped Thunder and Storm weren't to face their namesakes.

"That's what hats are for," George replied roundly, touching his topper. "I don't know why anyone puts a head on a curricle. How can one hope to be seen properly that way?"

Davies wondered who George expected to see them at all given the sparsity of habitation, but he kept his peace and the weather remained neither fair nor foul.

The farther they traveled from London, the more buoyant George became. Though he'd ceased to natter about horses, he grinned and waved at the few people they passed. For his part, Davies felt close to nodding off. Though the road had its bumps, the curricle made for a relatively smooth ride (Davies had to admit George kept a dab hand on the reins), and paired with fitful sleep and early rising, Davies was in want of rest.

He must have dozed, for he next became aware of the curricle rolling to a stop. Davies opened his eyes to see a small town stretching out before them.

George answered before he could ask. "Birchmere," he said. "The closest town to Montcliffe."

Montcliffe? Davies blinked sleep from his eyes. "But we're not going to Montcliffe. We're going to Faebourne."

"Except we don't know where Faebourne is," George pointed out. "So we must find someone who does."

Davies gestured at the road ahead of them that cut through the town. "Anyone here might be able to tell us. We don't have to go to Montcliffe."

George smiled in a way Davies didn't entirely trust. "Don't you want to see it? Aren't you at all curious about the place your mother grew up?"

Davies thought of the stories his mother had told him—always fairy tales, never truths. He'd asked her now and then about her family, but she had only ever smiled sadly and shaken her head. "I'd trade all of them for you," she once told him. That was the most she'd ever said on the subject.

Well, and I guess she did trade them for me. For my father first, but in the end, just me. He wondered whether she could have introduced him to her family after his father died. Had she considered it? Had she been too proud and angry to go back? Or had she perhaps tried—maybe written—and been turned away?

"I don't want to meet them," Davies said.

"It's not like they'll recognize you," said George. "Unless..." He tilted his head appraisingly. "Do you look like your mother?"

Davies scowled, but George only continued to study his face as though expecting the answer to present itself. "I don't know," Davies finally told him. "She was fair, and I am not. But I've been told my smile is the same as hers. And my chin."

"No time to grow a beard," George said. "We'll just have to hope no one makes the connection."

"No, we don't, because we're not going to Montcliffe," said

Davies. "Look there, a perfectly good inn. We can rest the horses, eat, get directions, and be on our way."

George huffed. "You're as bad as Duncan. Where's your sense of adventure?"

"My sense of adventure, such as it is, does not extend to painful memories. Nor, would I think, does Mr. Oliver's, which is almost certainly why he has not invited you to Dove Hill!"

George rocked back where he sat as though slapped, and Davies suppressed the immediate urge to apologize. Why should he? George was the one in the wrong, attempting to exploit Davies' past for his own amusement. Yet the hurt expression on George's face made Davies want to make amends all the same. He clamped his teeth against the impulse.

Without another word, George set the horses in motion again, rolling to a stop in front of the inn Davies had pointed out. The faded, weather-streaked red and gold sign announced it as the Crown and Cups. George hopped down from the curricle with no hint of the stiffness Davies felt after the journey; it took the valet slightly longer to unfold and ease himself to the ground. By the time he had, George had already handed the reins to the stable boy and gone inside.

Davies followed slowly, uncertain about the turmoil that welled inside him. George Fitzbert was not his friend, after all; they'd only been thrown together by circumstance. Once they retrieved Mr. Oliver, Davies would return to being nothing worth George Fitzbert's attention. The only reason he had George's attention now, Duncan Oliver notwithstanding, was that George found Davies' family history interesting, and George lacked entertainment.

Right. That was all there was to it. No reason for agitation. Davies hardly possessed the power to wound George's feelings. Only people you cared about could truly hurt you.

Davies pushed open the door, revealing an empty tavern save George and the portly man behind the bar whom Davies took to be the innkeeper. George sat at the bar, a smile on his face as he regaled the man with some story. From the back, a young woman entered carrying mugs of ale and two plates with an assortment of cold cuts of chicken and venison. She was lovely, with brown hair and a slender neck, and as George transferred his smile to her she lit up with one in return that made her a dozen times more beautiful. But George did not seem to notice. His attention slid instead toward the threshold where Davies continued to stand, and Davies fancied George grimaced before setting his smile back in place.

The lass turned to see what—or who—had captured George's eye, and when she spotted Davies her mouth fell open. "Papa!"

A bolt of confusion laced with panic shot through Davies. "I'm not your—"

But then the innkeeper looked up, too, and his face whitened. "M'lord," he said with an awkward half-bow. "How can we serve you?"

"I'm not—" Davies began again, but George's laughter overrode him.

"Well!" George managed once he mastered his voice. "I'd say there must be some family resemblance after all!"

aebourne's kitchen was partially subterranean. Duncan wondered whether it might have once been a cellar of some kind. *Maybe even a dungeon?* But he shook that thought aside. The walls were stone, the ceiling high and held with thick beams. Near the ceiling were long, horizontal windows to let in the slanting afternoon light.

Both Richard and Edward were already at work by the time Adelia led Duncan into the space, which was filled with long wooden tables. A sink stood against one wall, a large hearth took up all of another. Open cupboards held dishes, pots, and the like. All was tidy, but the place appeared abandoned. Where was the staff? Yet none of the Milnes seemed surprised or dismayed by the absence of their servants. The only thing that visibly upset Richard was the sight of Adelia's arm looped through Duncan's; as they entered the kitchen, he looked up from the pile of grass at his table and scowled.

If Adelia noticed her brother's displeasure, she chose to ignore it. "Ah!" she said brightly, "you've started!"

"The sooner done, the sooner he can go home," Richard said.

"I've finished mine!" Edward called from a table farther down.

Adelia tugged Duncan's arm. "Come, try it on."

He had little choice but to follow, though he felt Richard's sharp gaze driving into his shoulder blades as they passed him.

Edward, meanwhile, stood waving something at them that blurred before Duncan's eyes until Edward dropped it onto the table. "It's a shoe," Duncan realized. "Made of grass."

In truth, it was something of a marvel in the way the grass had been neatly woven to create the slipper. Duncan started to ask how Edward had done it so well and so quickly, but then Adelia picked it up and handed it to Duncan. "Try it," she said again.

He accepted the shoe and glanced around, but no chair or stool presented itself. So, not knowing how fragile a grass slipper might be, he gently set it on the floor and slid his right foot into it.

"Well?" Edward asked, his tone breathy with anticipation.

"It fits," Duncan said, once again in awe of the thing. It was more comfortable than he'd expected, though he supposed it usually wasn't unpleasant to walk on grass.

"And here is the other," Richard said. His voice so close behind him made Duncan hop with surprise; for a big man, Richard moved quietly. The second slipper landed with a slap on the floor beside Duncan's unshod left foot, and Duncan obligingly put it on. Though slightly larger than the right shoe, it didn't seem in any danger of falling off.

Aloysius, who Duncan had not realized was there, strolled over and sniffed at the handmade footwear. Then he sat down and looked up at Adelia, who in turn clasped her hands and with a wide grin pronounced, "Perfect!

"Now," she went on, "the cauldron."

"C-cauldron?" Duncan asked.

"A kind of pot," Adelia explained.

"No, I know what—" Duncan began but became distracted when Edward brought over a black, lidded bit of old iron from the cupboard shelf.

"It's not very big," Edward said, as though that were in the pot's favor. "So not too heavy."

The cauldron was roughly the size of a teapot, with a handle curving over the top and three small stubs that acted as feet for it to stand on. "Are we making soup?" Duncan asked. The pot didn't seem big enough to hold more than a ladleful for each of them.

"Oh," Adelia said, Duncan's question seeming to have kindled a thought in her. "We should probably eat something before you go. Can't send you out on an empty stomach."

"We *could*," Richard murmured.

"But we won't," Adelia said. She glanced around the kitchen then looked down at Aloysius. "We'll take tea in the Green Room," she said, then over her shoulder added, "Edward, bring the cauldron."

Feeling he had few options in the matter, Duncan followed Adelia and Richard (who had managed to put himself between his sister and their guest) back upstairs with Edward behind. The shoes slid a bit as Duncan walked, but no more than his stocking feet had. Still, he held the bannister tightly as they climbed.

They straggled back into the entry like an awkward line of ill-trained soldiers, and Adelia crossed the hall to a set of double doors. The Green Room, Duncan presumed, and upon its being revealed he saw that, indeed, it was. All of it, completely green. From the juniper-colored rug, to the basil paper hangings on the walls, to the very light coming through the windows—green.

Duncan paused on the threshold and tried to make sense of what he saw. The room ran the length of the house from front to back, with windows on three sides. Tall ones, like in the dining room. But the glass was crowded by the trees growing so close to the house, giving the light its greenish cast.

Opposite the doors, in the center of the outside wall, stood a modest fireplace of white marble, the only relief from the oppressive monotony of color. Dark furniture upholstered in (what else?) green were assembled in front of it: two settees facing one another, two armchairs with small tables at their sides. This collection appeared absurdly small in the massive room, like a herd of frightened cattle clustered in a huge meadow.

It was a room designed for parties and balls, though why the Milnes needed such a space baffled Duncan as they professed to never have guests.

Behind him, Richard cleared his throat, and Duncan realized he'd stopped in the doorway. He hastened into the room and, after seeing Adelia settled on a settee, took a seat in one of the chairs. Edward sat beside his sister, setting the cauldron on the floor near his feet. Richard chose the second chair.

The green light made the room somewhat gloomy. Duncan felt he had to squint to see, though Adelia's smile was bright enough. "Tea should be here any—"

Aloysius pranced in, and for a moment Duncan thought perhaps the fox would be carrying yet another basket, this time filled with teacups and who knew what else. But no. Instead, a somewhat blank-eyed footman pushed a tea cart in after him. Aloysius sat at Adelia's feet, and the footman stopped the cart in front of her then turned and left without a word.

"Is he mute?" Duncan wondered aloud.

"We never know who we're going to get," said Edward.

Duncan opened his mouth to ask then thought better of it. Asking questions at Faebourne had proven futile. Doing so only created more questions.

Adelia hummed to herself as she brewed and poured tea, which Duncan accepted strong and with only a little milk. He also took the scone Adelia offered—still warm! though how that was possible considering they'd just left an empty kitchen he could not fathom—his stomach reminding him it had been some time since breakfast.

Once everyone had been served, Aloysius looked up at Adelia and she sighed. "Yes, I suppose we do have to explain," she said. Then she turned to Duncan.

"Those shoes will allow you to get past the..." She paused to find the proper word. "Barriers that my mother's curse has raised against you. Now that it knows your reason for being here, it will attempt to hold you in as it does me. But if you wear those slippers, you can fool the..." Her gaze trailed toward the tree-crowded windows.

Duncan followed her line of sight then looked down at his newly manufactured footwear. "Then why don't you make some for yourself?"

"You saw what happens," Richard growled before Adelia could answer. "Slippers won't stop that."

"It's all right, Richard," said Adelia, "You can't expect him to understand all this. He hasn't lived with it as we have."

"You've given him shoes, and now he'll probably run off back to London." Richard eyed Duncan speculatively.

Duncan prided himself on being reasonable, civil. But it had been a long day and he was tired and confused and still a little hungry. He scowled at Richard. "You seem to want me here and not want me here all at the same time, Mr. Milne," he said. "Which is it?"

"I only wish you were not necessary," said Richard, "or that..." But then he pressed his lips into a line so thin they all but disappeared.

Edward took up the thread, speaking in his typically candid way. "My brother wishes you'd been less attractive. Or that it had been someone else at the club. You see, we were instructed—" Here he glanced down at Aloysius as though for confirmation or permission. "We were instructed to bring back the first man we met at the club on that Friday. And that was you!" Edward's cherubic face and sparkling eyes made it clear he did not share his brother's preference for some other hero. He gazed at Duncan with open admiration.

Duncan said, "As pleased as I have been to make your acquaintance, and to see your beautiful home, I can only agree that I do wish I'd left the club a little earlier."

For a brief moment Richard appeared startled, but then he cracked a small smile and inclined his head in acknowledgement. Duncan felt the tension in the room ease like heat dissipating in the face of a breeze.

"Well, then," said Adelia, "you'll have your chance to escape, so to speak. Though I sincerely hope you choose to return."

"Return from what exactly?" Duncan asked.

"In order to perform the ritual necessary to break the spell, we need to collect a few items." Adelia glanced at each of her brothers. "Richard and Edward have tried, but of course the curse prevents them from helping me."

Of course, thought Duncan. Aloud he said, "Am I to use the cauldron to collect these items?"

Edward reached down and lifted the pot for Duncan's inspection. "It's iron, you see."

"Yes," said Duncan, though what that had to do with anything he could not comprehend.

"There's a song," said Adelia, "that you need to capture."

"What, like sheet music?" Duncan asked.

"No," Adelia said. "It's a song. In the woods. You'll know it when you hear it."

"You must stay on the path," Richard added.

"If I'm understanding correctly," said Duncan, "you plan to send me off into the woods with a cauldron to search for a song that I will then somehow catch in the cauldron?"

"We'll send you with a picnic basket, too," Adelia said. "In case you are out for very long and miss dinner."

Duncan scanned their faces. Surely they were bamming him. *George!* he thought. *George has set all this up as a lark of some kind. He always did have too much time on his hands.*

But if his hypothesis were true, they were very good actors. Adelia and Edward appeared aglow with earnestness, and Richard watched narrowly as though in anticipation of Duncan's refusal.

"Well, then," said Duncan, rising and taking the cauldron from Edward, "I suppose I should make use of the remaining daylight."

CHAPTER 14

Davies remained frozen where he stood. "I'm not a lord," he said.

The innkeeper and his daughter exchanged glances. "But surely you're here from Montcliffe?" the man asked.

"No," said Davies. He spared a glare for the red-cheeked George, who held his hand in front of his mouth to stifle his laughter.

"The resemblance is extraordinary," the innkeeper insisted.

"There is some relation," George said, recovering his voice. "Mr. Davies here is the son of Lady Georgiana Lyming."

Glares clearly did not have any effect on George Fitzbert. Davies set his teeth and walked to the bar to join his traveling companion. The innkeeper's daughter scuttled aside, goggling at him as he passed.

"Begging your pardon," she said, and she dipped into a small curtsey as Davies' attention settled on her, "but we thought Lady Georgiana passed away some years ago."

"She did," Davies told her. He eyed the plate of cold cuts but his appetite had fled.

"I mean," the young lady went on, bobbing again when Davies looked up, "we hadn't heard she'd—"

"Lucy," her father said sharply.

"Ah," George said, "I think I understand. Lord Montcliffe put it about that his daughter had died. *Before* marriage or children."

"I don't know anything about it," said Davies. He took a sip of ale.

"Have you come to see Lord Montcliffe?" Lucy asked.

"Lucy," her father said again, "there is work enough to be done in the kitchen. Get on with you." As Lucy hastened away, the innkeeper said, "I apologize, gentlemen. We don't get many of your like around these parts. I have tried to teach her manners, but without means for practicing 'em..."

George nodded and waved away the man's excuses. "Is Montcliffe near here?"

"Through town, down the valley and up the hill. You can see it once you make the other side of town." The man frowned, and Davies could tell he wanted to say more but wasn't sure whether he should. Instead he drew a loaf of brown bread and a knife from under the bar and began to slice it with neat, quick strokes.

"It hardly matters," Davies said. "We're actually looking for Faebourne. Do you know where it is?"

The innkeeper's frown deepened and his brow furrowed. "We know *of* it, of course, but I can't say as I've ever known anyone to go to or come from there. The Milnes keep to themselves. They don't entertain," he finished, his expression weighted with meaning.

"They must have servants," George said, "people who come into town to do the shopping and whatnot, eh?"

But the man shook his head. "Not this town."

"Are we headed in the right direction?" Davies asked, endeavoring to keep the despair from his voice. He hated the thought they may have wasted their time in going the wrong way.

The man turned to regard him and again seemed discomfited by Davies' appearance; he began yet another bow but stopped himself short. "You'll want to go north from here. If you head into town and turn left at the church, you'll be pointed the right way." He hesitated. "You don't plan to visit Montcliffe?"

"I didn't even learn I was a relation until yesterday," said Davies. He forced himself to place some venison on a thick slice of bread and nibble at it; if he didn't eat now, he'd regret it later.

The innkeeper appeared troubled, and Davies looked away. The place was shabby but clean, clearly well run. Yet also sadly deserted. Leaded panes allowed in watery sunlight. Davies wondered whether the local patrons might not appreciate the daylight. Birchmere was far enough outside of anywhere not to get many visitors from afar, though perhaps coaches came through regularly enough. Still, steady business in the barroom would depend largely on the town's residents.

"It's not my place," the innkeeper said, his tone pitched low, "but seeing as Lord Montcliffe has been ill..."

"Ill?" George asked, and Davies looked over at him sharply.

"You can see why we thought you might be here to visit the estate," the man continued.

"We're not," Davies told him firmly.

But George asked, "Who is the next nearest relative? Drat, if only Henry were here. He'd know."

The innkeeper opened his mouth, but Davies said, "It doesn't matter who the next nearest relative is. At least, not to me."

And the innkeeper turned back to him, mouth open to reply, but George said, "You don't think he'd forgive you? For your mother's sake?"

And now the innkeeper just stood there, mouth agape, watching the conversation unspool.

"Forgive me?" Davies asked. "For what, existing? It is *I* who won't forgive *him*." And he stood up and marched back out of the tavern.

HE'D HAD the boy hitch the horses and was sitting in the curricle when George emerged some little while later. Davies studied his expression for a sign of whether he might be irritated, amused—any indicator of George's mood. But George only appeared weary as he climbed up to take his seat.

"Faebourne then?" George asked, taking up the reins, and Davies noted George kept his gaze straight ahead and would not look at him.

"Yes."

George gave a curt nod and urged Thunder and Storm into a trot without another word.

CHAPTER 15

*T*hey'd given him a greatcoat because, as Adelia had put it, "It's April, and the evenings are still quite cool." All well and good, but Duncan soon discovered that grass slippers did nothing to keep the cold from one's feet—or the wet, for that matter. Not that he went splashing into any puddles, but the forest floor was damp with spring and sundown.

When they'd been outside earlier that afternoon, Duncan had not seen any path like the one Richard had insisted he stay on, but upon leaving—a small, light hamper in one hand, a small, heavy cauldron in the other—he couldn't understand how he'd missed it. The trees arched over the worn dirt track that bent into the twilight, that odd gloaming peculiar to dusk causing the path to seem almost to glow despite the lack of direct light.

"A song," Duncan sighed to himself. "I'll know it when I hear it."

Not for the first time he wondered whether the entire Milne family might be touched in their heads. Could he stay out for a bit and then come back claiming to have caught the song? Would they know the difference? In short, was this a true quest or just a bit of playacting?

Duncan didn't know, and he didn't know *how* to know, either. *Even if I hear this song*, he thought, *how does one* catch *a song?* And then: *Why am I even taking this seriously?*

As instructed, he stayed on the path. Not out of superstition so much as practicality; venturing off the path would surely end with him lost and farther from home than ever. Still, progress was sluggish. The shoes were not sturdy and his hands were full, slowing him. And as the sun sank somewhere behind the trees, the canopy overhead and forest around him grew darker. Only the semi-luminescent path remained visible.

Duncan trudged onward, his arms feeling heavier with every stride. *I should go back*, he thought. Either he'd convince them he'd caught the song—if he could bring himself to lie, which he wasn't persuaded he could—or he'd suggest starting fresh in the morning. What had made them think going out so close to sunset was a good idea to begin with? He should have known better, even if they didn't.

So deciding, he turned around.

The path wasn't there.

He turned to look ahead of him, the way he'd been traveling. The trail gleamed faintly, showing the way.

Back. Nothing.

Duncan took a few stumbling steps toward the dark, but the track itself was not just lightless, it was gone. Where the flattened dirt had been, roots now crept and stones jutted. Even in boots, it would have been hazardous; in grass slippers, impossible.

"Perhaps this is why they chose evening," Duncan muttered, turning back toward the dim glimmer. "It surely doesn't glow in daylight." *Still*, he thought, *a lantern would have been more useful than a cauldron. Easier to carry, too.*

Resigned, he carried on, trying not to worry about how he would get back to Faebourne, or *if* he would get back to Faebourne. Maybe he would come across a village and get assistance in returning to London... But the thought of Adelia waiting hopefully for him... And he'd promised to help, after all. He was nothing if not a man of his word.

A low moan stopped Duncan mid-stride. He whipped his head right then left in an attempt to locate the sound. Then he looked down.

His stomach was growling.

How long had he been walking? Duncan looked up, but under the trees it was impossible to tell the time. No light broke through the branches. Full dark, he supposed, but that only meant it was night and not yet daybreak. There were a lot of hours in between.

Duncan glanced around, wishing for a place to sit, even if only a large rock of some kind. He didn't particularly relish the idea of settling on the ground. He could eat standing, perhaps, though he'd prefer to relieve his legs.

Then he saw it.

A bench.

In the middle of a forest?

But he didn't want to question it, this answer to his silent prayer.

It was a perfectly ordinary wooden garden bench, or so it seemed given the dimness of the illumination. The only light came from the dubious glow of the path.

Without further thought, Duncan stepped over and sat down, freeing his legs and arms from their chores as he set the cauldron down by his feet and the hamper on the bench beside him. As his stomach rumbled again, Duncan opened the basket and pulled out a hunk of bread and another of cheese and began to eat with gusto, glad to be alone and therefore unbeholden to etiquette. He was just rummaging through the basket in search of the jar of lemonade when he heard it.

Music.

Duncan sat up straight and strained his ears, scanning the darkness beyond the path, though he privately ridiculed himself for it. After all, one couldn't see a song.

What he did see, however, was another glow separate from that of the path, and brighter, too. It bounced around like a ball in the darkness on the other side of the trail. *Glow worm?* Duncan thought. But glow worms didn't float like this strange light that, upon reflection, was less like a ball and more like a feather caught in a breeze— it hovered then blew, hovered, dipped, then drifted closer as if propelled on a gust.

As it came nearer, it got larger. And the music grew louder.

By the time it reached the spot directly across from where he sat, what he'd first considered a glowing speck had elongated into a person. A woman, in fact. Humming and swaying as she walked.

"Miss Milne?" Duncan asked, confused. Because she looked remarkably like Adelia Milne, her effulgence an apparent byproduct of her very fair hair and skin reflecting the faint light of the path.

The young woman paused in her song and her step and smiled at him. Then her gaze dropped to where the cauldron sat beside Duncan's feet and the corners of her lips fell. "Why are you here?" she asked.

Despite the somewhat severe tone, her voice struck Duncan like a chord, as though the words she spoke were music themselves. The tune of them was sad, like a ballad, or a snatch of childhood lullabye that he couldn't quite remember. He found himself leaning forward, drawn, wanting her to speak again.

"I don't know," Duncan admitted. All at once he felt helpless and stupid. He wasn't meant for adventure; his was a life of books and the occasional card party, a ball here and there. Forests didn't enter into it, much less whatever he was doing there, and of that he still wasn't sure.

What would I do if this were London? he asked himself then answered by standing and giving a small bow. "Forgive my manners," he said. "May I be so forward as to introduce myself?"

The woman took a startled step backward when he rose and stared at him with wide, pale eyes. Duncan felt as though she were searching for something in his face. "All right," she said.

"Duncan Oliver," he said with another bow.

She smiled again. "Odette," she said, and when Duncan looked a question at her, "It is the only name I have."

"May I suggest, Miss Odette, that walking alone through dark forests is perhaps not the safest way to spend your evening?"

She pursed her perfectly rose pink lips at him. "I'm entirely safe barring any strange men carrying iron cauldrons. I'd say, in fact, I am more safe alone with myself than alone with you."

Duncan was tempted to point out that being with him meant she wasn't alone but chose to pursue the greater point. "I promise I am no threat to you, Miss Odette."

"Then why do you have that?" She pointed at the pot.

He grimaced, feeling foolish. The errand, after all, defied explanation, but he tried anyway. "I'm supposed to catch a—oh," he said, realizing. "*You're*... a song?"

"I am always a song, and I am sometimes a person," she told him.

"You look remarkably like someone I know," Duncan said. She was just Adelia's height, too, and had her hair piled and curled in the same way. Odette's movements and voice, however, were utterly different—her gestures no less graceful but more expansive, her speech *plus forte* yet more lilting, creating peaks and valleys of sound.

"All songs look like someone you know," she told him. "Or places. Some days I'm whole fields of flowers." Her gaze became distant and unfocused, her face alight and wistful. "Those are nice days."

It dawned on Duncan that he'd ceased to be amazed by the inexplicable. If anything, the bizarre had become normal for him in the course of the past few hours. "Are you every song?" he asked. "Or a particular song?"

"I'm many," she said, "but not all. It's difficult to explain." She glanced again at the cauldron, her expression pinched with wariness.

"I only need one, you see," said Duncan. "But I don't know which one. It would be a great help to me, and to the young lady that you remind me of."

"That answers your question then," said Odette. "The song you need is the one that reminds you of her. The one that makes me this." Her hands fluttered over her person, indicating herself. "I would give it to you, but..."

"Would it hurt? If you gave me a song?" Duncan asked.

"No. But to put even part of me in there..." She nodded at the pot. "It would sap me of much of my..." She put a finger to her chin as she sought the word she wanted.

"Power?" Duncan prompted.

Odette shook her head, her curls bouncing. "It's not power, exactly," she said. "Not in the way you mean. Effectiveness is the only way I can think of to describe it."

Duncan slumped where he stood. He had no idea whether the song needed to be "effective" for the Milnes to make use of it. But surely they would not have given him the cauldron if it might harm the very thing they required? Or maybe they didn't know.

Another look at Odette's sorrowful countenance decided him. He refused to risk damaging her, whatever or whomever she may be.

"Maybe there is no need for the cauldron," he suggested.

Odette grew still, eyes wide and watchful like a deer sensing danger.

"That is," Duncan continued, "perhaps you could simply come back with me? I don't know why they need you," he blundered on, "but I've promised to help them—"

"A promise is a very sacred thing," said Odette solemnly.

"Yes, and I—that is, she's got a curse on her and will turn into a beast—it's an enfield apparently—so I said I'd help, and then they told me to come catch a song." He stopped for breath and to consider. "I don't know how that's supposed to help, actually."

"Songs help most things," Odette said. Suddenly her face lit up. "Potent!" she said. "That's the word!" She ducked her head in a coy way. "I'm much better with musical notes than words."

"Potent," Duncan echoed thoughtfully, as though tasting the word. It sounded better in Odette's mouth than his, but he wagered most anything would sound lovely in that melodic voice. "Yes, maybe that's why they need it. Will you come?" he asked.

Odette nibbled her lip, her gaze returning to the cauldron.

"We can leave it," Duncan offered, "if you like." Privately, he hoped that would be acceptable to the Milnes. If the pot was sacred in some way, he'd come back for it later.

Odette's periwinkle eyes met his. After a moment she gave a decisive nod. "Very well. But don't forget your hamper."

Duncan turned and hooked the basket onto his arm. Odette

then stepped over to take his other. She was, he thought, a much more pleasant burden, so to speak, than the cauldron had been.

When they turned back toward Faebourne, the roots and stones were gone, and the way illuminated as though by a carpet of starlight.

CHAPTER 16

They rode through Birchmere in silence, Davies soon wishing he'd eaten more or at least taken a longer rest from the jolting curricle. Still, he gritted his teeth and said nothing until the church the innkeeper had spoken of came into view. When George showed no sign of turning as per the directions, Davies yelped, "Wait!"

George obliged him by drawing the horses to a halt across the road from the church. It was not particularly large, Davies observed, but built of weathered grey stone and potentially quite old.

"Well?" George asked, and Davies turned from his idle scrutiny of the house of worship. He only wanted not to have to look George in the eye, although he wasn't sure why. George was the one at fault, after all, pursuing a line of enquiry that Davies had made clear he had no interest in. The idea of George using his past to amuse himself set Davies' blood to boil again.

"The innkeeper said to turn at the church." Davies pointed to the street perpendicular to the one they were on. "That is north, I believe."

A woman carrying a basket on her arm, her other hand holding tightly to a little girl's, hurried past the curricle. Both ogled—the girl pointing to the horses, the woman's dark and glistening eyes on him. She stared until Davies thought her head might turn completely backward on her neck. But no, a near collision with a young man forced the woman to return her attention to her immediate surroundings.

"And that," said George, recalling Davies to the immediate moment, "is Montcliffe."

Davies' gaze followed the line of George's thrusting finger. The church was, as churches were often wont to be, at the high point of the town, meaning from where the curricle sat, he and George could see the gradual dip of Birchmere as it flowed through the valley. And as Birchmere went down, another hill rose beyond upon which stood a towering manor that could easily have been mistaken for a castle. The stone on Montcliffe was a warmer, more buttery shade than the grey of the church but the building itself far more foreboding. Its peaks and chimneys stabbed at the clouds as though to cut them open, though whether to make them bleed sun or rain could not be determined. Perhaps the act of violence was all Montcliffe desired, and the result not of consequence to it.

Davies shook his head at the dark thoughts. This house he'd never known, never consciously been connected to, and yet it had such immediate effect on him. The shivers down his back and arms only reinforced his resolve to go in another direction entirely.

"What of it?" he asked.

With a sigh, George dropped his arm and took up the reins. "I only thought—"

Just then a young gentleman stepped up to Davies' side of the curricle and touched his hat. "Begging pardon, but are you the new Lord Montcliffe?"

Davies looked down and recognized the man as the one the woman had nearly run headlong into. A youngish, middling gentleman in well-made but not spectacular clothes. "I'm not any Lord Montcliffe," Davies told him, "old, new, or otherwise."

"Oh, I think otherwise," muttered George, but Davies ignored him.

"But you must be!" the stranger protested. "That is, forgive me, but the resemblance, it can't be coincidence. And we've been expecting..." He stopped with a grimace.

"Whoever you're expecting, it isn't me," Davies said, not unkindly. Something about the man's mixture of hope and desperation moved the valet to pity. "We're only passing through."

But then George leaned forward and asked. "We who?"

"Oh!" The man touched his hat again. "I didn't see you. Pardon?"

"You said 'we've been expecting'," said George. "You and who else?"

The man glanced up and down the street. "Well, everyone."

"What, like the town?" George asked.

"More or less," said the man. "I'm Percy, by the way." This time he took the hat off for a full tip, complete with flourish. "Percy Harding."

"George Fitzbert," said George, "and the sour one is Davies. You're not mad, by the way. His mother was Lady Georgiana Lyming."

Percy's mouth became a little "o" of astonishment. "But Lady Georgiana—"

"Didn't die," George said. "Well..." His gaze bounced off Davies' glare. "She did die, but not when they said. She married and..." He gestured at Davies.

"So you *are* the new Lord Montcliffe!" Percy cried.

"I have nothing to do with Montcliffe," Davies insisted, all his former compassion fleeing in the face of his irritation. "We're looking for a friend of ours who left London quite abruptly."

Percy's brow furrowed. "And came to Birchmere?"

"We think he's at Faebourne," said Davies.

The "o" reappeared. "No one goes to Faebourne."

"You know where it is?" Davies asked.

Percy shook his head. "That way," he said, waving a hand at the road that traveled past the church. "Somewhere. That's all I or anyone knows about it."

Davies turned to George in triumph, but George's full attention remained on Percy. "Why is everyone so eager for a new Lord Montcliffe?"

Percy's fingers fluttered, and suddenly he seemed unable to

look Davies or George in the eyes. "Not eager so much as... concerned..."

"Concerned about what?" George pressed.

Percy did meet their gazes then, his expression anguished. "The current heir is... Well, that is, it's really not my place to—"

"We've heard Lord Montcliffe is ill," interjected George.

Percy nodded.

"Dying?" George asked.

Percy's throat bobbed as he swallowed and he nodded again.

George turned to Davies. "There you are then."

"No, I'm not," said Davies. "Even if I did want—and I don't —I've been disowned."

"He can't have disowned you if he never knew you existed," said George. "You should at least meet him before he kicks it."

"Clearly he's made arrangements for his succession," Davies said with a glance at Percy for confirmation. At Percy's nod, Davies added, "I see no reason to insert myself."

"Going to be a valet your whole life?" George asked, and Percy's eyes fairly popped.

"Valet?"

"It's his employer and my friend we're seeking," George told him.

Percy frowned. "Two people?"

"What? No," said George. "His employer *is* my friend."

"And still missing," Davies pointed out. His dark eyes met George's amber ones, and to Davies it felt like a duel. But at last George sighed and nodded.

"Yes, well, give our best to the rest of the town," George told Percy. "We hope you find a Lord Montcliffe that's to your liking." So saying, he turned Thunder and Storm northward, giving Percy no warning and little time to scuttle out of the way.

Davies glanced back just once to see Percy Harding still standing in the road, staring after them.

CHAPTER 17

Odette hummed as they walked, and Duncan's mind fuzzed with the sound. The dark trees seemed to sway in time, bending closer as though to reach the source of the music.

I'm overtired, Duncan thought. He hadn't slept all that well in the carriage ride to Faebourne, and the day had been a full one. Trees behaving oddly, grass slippers, beastly curses, a woman proclaiming to be a song... *Maybe I'm asleep right now.*

Usually, when Duncan realized in a dream that he was, in fact, asleep, he woke up at once. Alas, no such awakening occurred.

Beside him, Odette tugged his arm gently. "You are troubled."

He blinked at her, the words taking a moment to sink in past the lulling rise and fall of her voice. "No," he said.

"You slowed down. Don't you want to go back?"

"Yes," Duncan said, and they resumed their former pace. Before long, the darkness of trees retreated from the sides of the path and the hulk of the house came into view. But as they came to the edge of the lawn, Odette stopped.

"I can't," she said. "Not like this."

"You mean not looking like...?" Duncan asked.

Odette scanned the house; indeed, she seemed to scan the very air around it. "There's magic here."

Strangely enough, the declaration did not faze Duncan. "Is that bad?"

She looked down at his feet. "You have shoes for it. I do not."

Duncan looked down, too. The grass slippers had held up remarkably well all things considered. "Well, then," he said, "you can borrow mine." He stepped onto the lawn then toed off the shoes, picked them up, and handed them to Odette. "I needed them to get out there, but it seems you need them to get in here." He glanced around at the open air. "Wherever 'in here' is."

Odette smiled and likewise stepped out of her leather slippers. "I don't have to come in as a person," she said. "But I like being concentrated, all in one place. Otherwise I worry I might lose something important. They're a little big," she said as she put on the grass shoes, "but I do believe I'll be all right once I get inside." And she stepped onto the lawn.

Duncan held his breath and waited.

Odette stopped and waited, too, her wide eyes searching the sky for something Duncan could not see. After a moment she let out a little sigh and smiled. Duncan took it as a cue to begin breathing again. He offered Odette his arm and led her onto the veranda and into the house.

~

"OH!" said Odette when she spotted Aloysius in the entryway.

The fox sat with his tail curled around his black paws. His golden gaze traveled from Odette to Duncan, and Duncan supposed he could only be imagining the accusation he felt radiating from the russet beast.

Odette shuffled forward—the only way she could move in the oversized slippers was to scuff them along the floor—and began to hum. Aloysius transferred his attention back to her, and Duncan watched as Odette changed. Not all at once, no; in fact, Duncan almost didn't notice it at first. But the pale hair slowly darkened to a red-gold, and the white skin likewise became more peachy in tone. Her gown, which the lights of

Faebourne had revealed to be periwinkle in color, transmuted into pale blue.

She put a hand out toward Aloysius, but the fox laid his ears back. When Odette looked over at Duncan, he saw her eyes had turned a mossy green. "He does not like me."

"I'm sure that's not true," said Duncan. He looked at Aloysius, who stared back seemingly affronted by Duncan's presumption.

Odette waggled her fingers at Aloysius, but he leaned away and lifted a paw as though offended by the offer of her touch. In defeat, Odette dropped her arm. "I even changed to match his—"

An audible gasp slithered through the entry, sliding along the walls like an invisible serpent. Duncan turned to see Richard at the top of the stairs. "Who or what is this?" Richard demanded.

"This is—" Duncan began. "That is, she's the one who..."

Odette curtseyed as Richard stalked down the stairs. "I'm Odette." She straightened and smiled at him. "Thank you for your hospitality."

"Hardly," said Richard as he stopped nearly nose-to-nose with her. Well, Duncan reasoned, nose to forehead anyway, seeing as Odette was not nearly as tall. "Why do you look like—?"

"Mummy?"

Edward appeared in the Green Room doorway.

"No," Richard answered flatly.

Odette looked over her shoulder at Aloysius. "Is that who I'm supposed to be?"

"You look just like her," said Edward, taking small, reverent steps toward her.

"She... changes," Duncan explained. "But she's the—"

"Where is the cauldron?" Richard asked.

Duncan huffed and restrained his frustration. "That is what I'm trying to explain. She wouldn't fit in the cauldron."

"She?" Edward asked. His eyes did not leave Odette.

"Miss Odette. She's... a song. Or several songs. Or something. Isn't that what you sent me to retrieve?"

"You brought her in here without containing her?" Richard's voice was low and furious.

"Look," said Duncan, no longer hiding his own ire, "you asked me to bring you a song, and I did."

"In a cauldron! Which you didn't!"

"Miss Odette," said Duncan, "my shoes, if you please."

She blinked at him, and for a moment Duncan thought she hadn't heard. But then she nodded, stepped out of the slippers, and backed away from them to allow Duncan to put them on.

"What are you doing?" Richard demanded.

Duncan did not respond. He only walked to the front door of Faebourne, hefted it open, and exited into the night.

CHAPTER 18

*I*t grew dark faster than seemed natural. Davies
supposed it was the fault of the trees, which thickened
as they traveled north. The road, too, became more of a track,
uneven in places so that they bounced and jounced along most
uncomfortably.

No more comfortable was the silence and George's pinched
expression that Davies told himself was concentration rather
than anger. Thunder and Storm required strong and steady
hands, particularly given the unfavorable condition of the road.
Davies therefore chose to let George carry on without commen-
tary or conversation.

But then, as the sky became a dusky shade of heather,
George said, "Would you really rather be a valet than a lord?"

The words, though low, stung. "I'm a very good valet," Davies
answered stiffly.

George glanced at him. "That doesn't enter into it. To be at
someone else's beck and call at all hours—"

"Mr. Oliver is a fine employer."

"Yes, I'm sure he is. If anything, you're more like to manage
him than he is you. But wouldn't you rather have servants of
your own?"

"Not particularly."

George did more than glance at that; he stared and gaped. "Why not?"

"It would be boring," said Davies.

"Boring!" George echoed. "To give parties, and go to parties, and have whatever you want whenever you want it?"

"Is that what you have?" Davies asked.

"I'm not a lord!"

"But you are a gentleman, are you not?"

George's mouth snapped shut, and all at once Davies realized he had to squint to see him, the daylight having all but fled.

"I don't want to be chased by young ladies and their mamas just because I have a title," Davies went on. "Seems more trouble than it's worth."

George did not answer, and again Davies assumed his muteness was due to his need to give all attention to managing the horses now that the road was near impossible to see. Indeed, without lanterns they would be required to stop soon for the night; the horses surely wanted rest, too. Davies hoped a house or village would present itself so they would not have to lie rough in the woods. He didn't mind so much for himself, but it would be bad for the clothes.

As though in answer to his wish, the trees alongside the road drew back and the silhouette of a building appeared in the distance. The road went from dirt track to smoothed gravel, and after a little way Davies realized the way would end at the house, which grew larger by the second. "Is that Faebourne?" he wondered aloud.

"For a place no one seemed able to locate, it seems like a relatively direct route," said George. "Yet they say the staff never goes into town."

"Perhaps it's self-sustaining," Davies suggested.

"Growing vegetables, maybe, but slaughtering their own meat?"

"Maybe they don't eat meat."

"Maybe this isn't even Faebourne," said George. "Maybe we missed a turn somewhere."

But it *was* Faebourne; Davies felt oddly certain of it as the gravel rounded into a circle in front of the massive, gothic structure. And then:

"Duncan!" The Christian name came to Davies' lips first, all propriety shot down by surprise. It was dark out, but something in the shape of the man and the way he moved told Davies that it was his employer. Also that Duncan Oliver was, contrary to his typically placid nature, furious.

George stopped the curricle in front of the house and hopped down just as Duncan came to an abrupt halt short of the wheels. "What are you doing here?" Duncan asked in astonishment.

"We could ask the same of you," George told him.

But Duncan was squinting up at the curricle. "Davies?"

Davies unfolded his kinked body and joined the others as Duncan said, "Now you've done it."

"Done what?" George asked.

"You won't get out without shoes," said Duncan.

"We have shoes," Davies said. He peered at Duncan through the gathering gloom. "Are you well, sir?"

"Not those shoes," was all Duncan said. "Those shoes don't work here."

Professional curiosity aroused, Davies bent to try and see which shoes Duncan might be wearing and what made them "work," while George looked back up at the curricle. "Hmm," George said, "we clearly didn't consider having three on the way home."

Straightening, Davies looked at him. "We? You're the one who made the travel arrangements."

"Yes, well, it did occur to me you might stop at Montcliffe. What are you looking at?" George asked Duncan, who was frowning over his shoulder at the house.

"I thought at least one of them might come after me," said Duncan.

A stretch of silence settled over them, just long enough for Davies to notice the lack of country noises: no insects, no nightbirds, no breeze through the trees. Nothing. Even Thunder and Storm seemed to have stopped breathing.

Finally, George asked, "Did you want them to?"

"They said they needed me," Duncan said.

"For what?" asked George.

"At the very least, I should have taken proper leave of Miss Milne," Duncan went on. His shoulders slumped. "How ill-mannered of me."

"For God's sake, man," George huffed, "what in blazes is going on?"

Davies eyed Duncan a moment longer before adding, "And where did you get those clothes?"

CHAPTER 19

"*M*r. Oliver!"

The voice carried clearly on the still night air. Not sharp in tone, but not sweet either, Davies thought. He could only describe it as alarmed.

A woman followed the sound, so pale in every aspect that it almost seemed a star had fallen and taken human form. She hurried down the walk to where they stood and placed a hand on Duncan's arm.

Davies and George exchanged glances.

The lady, however, had eyes only for Duncan. "Where are you going?" she asked, and only then did she spare a look for the newcomers.

"I did my best," Duncan told her, and Davies had never heard him sound quite so petulant, not even when aggrieved by George's antics (a not uncommon occurrence). Then, with a gesture at the others, Duncan said, "Oh. May I present Mr. George Fitzbert and Mr. Owain Davies. Gentlemen, this is Miss Adelia Milne."

"The one you failed to take proper leave of," said George.

"Leave?" Adelia asked, her voice rising in pitch, and Davies wondered whether her alarm might become full hysteria.

"I brought the song," Duncan said, "just as you asked. Well, not *just* as you asked. But I could hardly ask her to crawl into a cauldron!"

Davies and George looked at one another again.

"Yes, thank you," Adelia said. "You must forgive Richard; it's been too much for him." She turned to George and Davies, pale blue eyes wide with a plea for understanding. "He's so used to our quiet life, you see," she told them. "To have all this upheaval..." She shook her head.

"But he wants you to get well doesn't he?" Duncan asked.

"Of course!" said Adelia.

"I'm sorry, but are you ill?" Davies ventured.

Adelia looked from Duncan to Davies and back again. Duncan said with an encouraging smile, "It's perfectly safe to tell Davies just about anything. I certainly do."

Adelia's mouth fell open just a little, and again her gaze darted between them. Davies immediately followed her line of thinking—some people were more perceptive than others, and Miss Milne had clearly extracted some assumptions from his employer's words. To smooth things, Davies offered somewhat abashedly, "I am Mr. Oliver's valet." He was gratified to see her shoulders ease.

"Oh," she said, "yes, Edward said he meant to bring you, too, but..." She shook her head again, this time in the way of an indulgent sister aiming to excuse a sibling's forgetfulness.

"What, he forgot to pack him?" George asked. His sharp tone startled Davies, and even Duncan threw him a surprised look. But Adelia took no notice. Returning her attention to Duncan, she said, "Please. Do come inside." She smiled to include George and Davies. "All of you. It's late, and your horses must need rest, even if you don't."

Seemingly out of nowhere, a lad appeared at Storm's head. The boy wore a lace-trimmed shirt, a velvet vest of corbeau green frogged in golden brown, and grey breeches topped by shiny black boots. If nothing else, Davies thought, the Milnes dressed their servants very well.

Davies realized George was frowning at him. Or perhaps at the young groom presuming to handle his horses. But no, Davies was sure the heat of George's amber gaze was directed at himself.

Now what have I done? He squelched the unease and forced pique into its place. *I have more right to be irritated with him than him with me. If he says one more thing about Montcliffe...*

"We'll have your bags brought in," Adelia assured them.

"They'll need shoes," Duncan mumbled as he allowed Adelia to steer him back toward the house.

Adelia glanced back. "They have shoes."

"Not like mine," said Duncan.

Davies caught George's eye, and for a moment neither of them moved, each silently challenging the other to go first. Finally, George sighed. "Once a servant, eh?"

Davies' patience broke. "*Why* are you so fixed on my social status? Is it because you don't have any? Can you simply not conceive of someone being happy as a valet? Do you honestly believe all your servants live in constant sorrow due to their place?"

George stopped and turned to face him. "We're very good to our servants," he said.

"And Mr. Oliver is very good to me," Davies told him. "He needs us—me, Wilkins, Mrs. Bentham, Bailey. We're his family. And they are mine."

"So is Montcliffe."

Davies shook his head. "I think true family is of our own making."

"Only people unhappy with their blood relatives ever say that," George said, turning around again. "If your mother—"

In two strides, Davies caught up to him. He grabbed George by the shoulder and spun him so they faced one another. "Stop. Bringing. Up. My. Mother."

To Davies' surprise, George did not answer ire with ire. Instead he appeared genuinely perplexed. "Aren't you proud of where you come from?"

Davies thought about it; he wanted to be truthful, and it wasn't a question he'd often pondered. "I'm. . . content with where I come from. And that isn't Montcliffe—you know I had no idea about that. A loving mother, and the little bit I remember of my father... That's enough."

George's face fell, not with disappointment so much as

sorrow. "Then you are very fortunate indeed," he said. And he turned away again toward the house.

Davies waited a respectful minute before following.

CHAPTER 20

*D*uncan no longer had expectations of any kind. He could not begin to predict what might happen next. In part, this frustrated him because he felt helpless to control events. But in part it was rather nice not to bear the weight of responsibility. At home, he made all the decisions. At Faebourne, he was wanted (at least by some), but his obligations were reduced. Go fetch a song? Done and done. The rest was up to the Milnes.

For the first time in his life, Duncan Oliver felt significant.

But not too significant.

It made for a nice balance.

When they stepped into the entry, it was empty. Duncan's sense of wellbeing morphed into wariness. "Where are they?"

"Dinner," Adelia said. "Oh, but we'll have to lay two more places..." She looked over her shoulder at the front door, which she'd left open a crack in the form of an invitation. "They *will* come inside, won't they?"

"George wouldn't miss it," Duncan replied absently, his attention straining toward the dining room. Anticipation crawled up his spine like a spider, though he couldn't have said what had him so on edge.

"He's the one you spoke of before," Adelia said. "The one who told you about us."

Duncan's disquiet was momentarily diverted. "He didn't know much to tell. When you come to London, you will be able to speak for yourself. People will be happy to meet you. All of you," he added.

Adelia smiled, albeit somewhat sadly. "You sound so certain."

"Certain?"

"That I will be able to go to London."

Before Duncan's spirits had time to plummet at her lack of faith—a doubt he feared was contagious—George pushed open the door. He removed his hat and glanced around. "So this is the legendary Faebourne."

Adelia tipped slightly to the left as though to see around him. "Where is your friend?"

"He's..." George glanced behind him. "Not my friend, I don't think."

Duncan had never seen George look quite so downtrodden. Perhaps the travel had worn him. As he tried to think of a light-hearted response to cheer his friend, Adelia answered, "Oh, but he is! I can tell."

George's brows lowered. "Can you? How?"

Davies slipped into the entry hall, forcing George to step aside and make room. Neither man looked at the other. If anything, by Duncan's estimation, they were working very hard at *not* looking at one another.

"There, you see," Adelia said. She turned her shining face up to Duncan's. "They like each other very much!"

Her enthusiasm was as infectious as her skepticism had been moments before, and Duncan could not help but smile back. But he still thought that Miss Milne's lack of social experience caused her to misread her guests' behavior.

"You must be hungry," Adelia said to George and Davies, then with another look at Duncan added, "all of you."

Davies cleared his throat. "We might better wash up a bit from our journey first."

"Oh! Yes! Aloysius can lead you up to your rooms." Adelia glanced around, and Duncan did likewise. As if by magic—and, Duncan was beginning to believe, very possibly exactly by magic

—the fox appeared at the foot of the stairs, sitting primly as though he'd been waiting there all the while.

"There you are!" Adelia cooed.

Duncan could not resist stealing a glance at George and Davies, who wore matching expressions of mistrust as they eyed the fox.

"Choose whichever rooms you believe will suit them," Adelia told her pet. "Wait for them, would you, and show them to the dining room when they're ready?"

George and Davies turned as one to Duncan. He nodded encouragement at them. "You have boots on, so no need to worry about your toes."

For his part, Aloysius turned in a coppery whirl and started up the stairs, pausing only once to look back and ensure his charges followed. Duncan would have gone with them, seen them settled, explained as best he could, but Adelia still had his arm and was tugging him toward dinner.

CHAPTER 21

*T*hey marched up after the fox in silence until George whispered, "Does it talk?"

"I don't think so," Davies murmured.

At the top of the stairs, Davies caught his breath. From outside, Faebourne stretched wide, though in the dark and because of the closeness of the trees, it had been impossible to tell just how wide. The corridor at the top of the stairs showed Faebourne's size clearly as it disappeared into darkness in either direction.

He ogled so long, he nearly lost sight of George and Aloysius, who had turned left and were making their way past any number of doors. Then, abruptly, the fox sat down outside one such door.

George and Davies stared at Aloysius. The fox stared steadily back.

"Is this mine or his?" George finally asked.

Aloysius cocked his head.

George looked to Davies. "I suppose we can go in and decide which of us wants it."

Davies nodded, and George pushed open the door.

The room had somehow already been prepared for guests. A merry blaze burned in the grate, giving the space a haunting glow as light flickered over the furnishings. But the linens were fresh, and a ewer of water stood warming on a table near the fireplace, a bowl and a towel at the ready. The sight of a cake of soap surprised Davies—he had not expected an isolated place such as Faebourne to have access to such a luxury—but he would hardly complain.

Aloysius pranced past in the firelight and went to stand by a door all but concealed in a shallow alcove on the far side of the jutting mantel. Without much thought, Davies walked over and opened the door. It led to a second bedroom, the mirror of the one they were in.

"Ah, I see. Adjoining rooms," Davies said.

George appeared at his shoulder, craning for a look. "Doesn't matter who sleeps where then, does it?"

For some reason, the dismissiveness of the statement vexed Davies. "Well then, I'll just—" He stepped into the second room and closed the door behind him. Much to his relief, a quick scan revealed another door that led to the hall; he would not be required to walk through George's room to enter and exit his own.

"You want that one, do you?" George called through the slab of polished wood.

"Clean yourself up," Davies directed, "else we'll miss dinner." He listened to the soft pad of George's steps as he moved away then went to splash some water on his face and wash his hands. *What I wouldn't give for fresh clothes.*

From the corner of the room came a long, low creak. Davies turned, stiff with alarm, then saw the wardrobe slowly opening. *They can't already have brought our bags.* Then again, they'd somehow readied the rooms in impossibly swift time. How large must the staff be for such an estate?

Hopeful that his bag might be there after all, he walked over to the wardrobe to investigate.

The cupboard revealed nothing familiar, not his bag nor his clothes. However, it did hold a full measure of garments, all of them quite fine. Unable to resist, Davies removed a jacket of deep blue kerseymere and an embroidered waistcoat. His trained eye suggested the clothes were almost exactly his fit. He reached next for a lawn shirt—simple but well made—and had just laid hands on a white satin cravat when a rap at the door connecting his room to George's caused him to jump.

George entered before Davies could answer the knock. "What are you doing? Oh, clothes. Are these yours?" He reached out to finger the jacket Davies had folded over the back of a chair.

"No," said Davies, "they were in the wardrobe."

George smiled in what Davies considered an oddly rueful way. "Ever the valet." Then he snapped to. "Do they fit?"

"I don't know."

"Let's find out! They look to be the correct size, eh? No use wasting them."

"We should go to dinner," said Davies, backing away from the clothes like a man avoiding the temptations of hell.

"It won't take but a minute," George insisted. "You of all people should be able to do it quickly. Oh! Do you think I have any?" George strode back toward the connecting door. "Come help me choose."

"I really don't understand you," Davies said to George's back. "Half the time you are dismayed that I am a valet, and the other half you are pleased by it."

"I only wish you were mine," George called back. "Duncan always looks natty. Oh, claret! My favorite color!"

"It makes you look ruddy," Davies muttered. He looked longingly at the clothes on the chair. It would be downright rude to wear someone else's clothes. Well, someone else's that hadn't been specifically gifted to him.

"Does it really?" George said from the doorway, making Davies jump again. He turned and saw George had put on the jacket, which fit him precisely. But George was frowning, his amber eyes tight with concern.

"Hasn't *your* valet told you that?"

"I don't have one," said George. "Mum says that, as I have Henry and he has me, there's no use hiring one."

Davies considered that for a moment. "I suppose your brother would not want to hurt your feelings." That did fit in with what he'd witnessed of Henry Fitzbert's personality. "But what happens when one of you gets married?"

"He doesn't give a fig about my feelings, he just knows I don't value his opinion," said George, turning back to his room. "And neither of us is likely to marry. Though for rather different reasons." This last was uttered as a seeming afterthought while George pulled a carmelite jacket loose from the press of the wardrobe. "How about this one?"

"Do you value *my* opinion?"

"I wouldn't ask if I didn't."

"Why?"

"Hmm?" George shrugged out of the deep red and slipped on the dark brown.

"Why do you value my opinion? You hardly know me."

"I told you. Duncan always looks top notch. You clearly know your game."

"Well, then, yes. That one suits you far better," Davies told him.

"Go on, then," George said. "Get dressed." Davies hesitated, but then George delivered the deciding blow: "It would be ill-bred to go to dinner in your travel clothes."

Davies went back into his room and kicked the door closed behind him, muffling George's parting shout: "And then come help me with my cravat!"

CHAPTER 22

*D*uncan sat on the edge of his chair at the head of the table, Adelia Milne to his left and Odette on his right. Richard glared at him from the other side of his sister. Edward, situated beside Odette, gazed at her with undisguised enchantment.

But was it infatuation or literal enchantment? Duncan realized either was possible.

A half dozen times, Duncan opened his mouth with the intention of breaking the awkward silence as they waited for George and Davies. But each time, he could think of nothing to say and ended up snapping his jaw shut again.

At last, Aloysius trotted in with the tardy guests at his heels. "So sorry for taking so long," George said without preamble. He dropped into the chair next to Richard, and Davies—with decidedly more grace—took the seat opposite, next to Edward. Almost immediately, footmen appeared and began serving. Duncan glanced around for some kind of hidden doorway that allowed the staff to materialize so quickly and silently, but he could see nothing. He supposed it must be well hidden indeed.

Edward broke free of his enrapturement with Odette just long enough to survey the newcomers. "Why, this is the most people we've ever had in this room!" he exclaimed.

George took in the oversized room with a frown. "Really?"

"We normally dine much earlier too," Richard said pointedly. George only nodded. "Country hours and all that, I suppose." Davies lowered his head over his soup.

"It won't be very fancy, I'm afraid," Adelia put in. "We aren't typically formal here."

"It's normally just us," Edward added. His colorful gaze took in the numerous guests, and Duncan noted he fairly juttered with eagerness. *Like an excited puppy*, Duncan thought, and he felt a sudden warmth for this young man, so innocent and happy despite all the odd circumstances encasing him. *Well, he doesn't know any better or any different.* But Duncan suspected even if Edward Milne had a broader knowledge of the world, he wouldn't approach it any differently. An optimist, was Edward, always trusting things would work out and that those around him would behave honorably.

All at once, Duncan understood Richard's surliness. To be charged with ushering Edward and Adelia through the world would be a taxing task. If the two younger Milnes were pups, Richard was the wolf guarding them. Faebourne was their den, then, a heretofore impregnable fortress. Only concern for his sister's condition had prompted Richard to permit an outsider—even going so far as to leave the sanctuary of home and fetch one. Yet with Duncan had come more outsiders. Duncan felt sure that, to Richard, he must seem like a cure worse than the disease.

"You're not eating," Adelia chided gently.

Duncan snapped out of his meandering thoughts to discover Adelia's bright blue eyes directed at him. "Sorry," he said, and hastily took a gulp of the onion soup.

"We should be the ones apologizing," said Adelia. "I am so sorry that Richard—" She glanced at her eldest brother. "He was only startled, you see."

Duncan risked a peek at the stone-faced eldest Milne and could not imagine him being startled by anything, ever. He kept that thought to himself and turned to Odette, who hummed and stirred her soup, oblivious to the intensity of Edward's attention. Duncan likewise caught Davies frowning slightly in Edward's direction and George frowning rather more markedly across the table at Davies. *What the devil is going on with those two?* More specifically, Duncan wondered how his valet and his best friend —two people he would never have paired, for what cause would they have to cross paths?—conspired to come find him, but that was a story he would have to wait to hear.

"Don't you like onion soup, Miss Odette?" Edward asked solicitously when she failed to notice his silent earnestness.

"It's pretty," she said, continuing to swirl the broth with her spoon. She looked up and caught Edward's searching gaze. "Oh, but songs don't eat, of course." She inhaled deeply. "It smells nice anyway."

Duncan watched Odette smile shyly at Edward and him smile back, and his stomach clinched in a way that at first made him think the soup had disagreed with him. Then he realized he was witnessing the bloom of love. The clinch became a tight fist in Duncan's abdomen, though he wasn't sure why.

Footmen whisked the soup away and pigeon appeared almost simultaneously, accompanied by sorrel and radishes. Davies' primness caught Duncan's eye; for a valet, his manners were prettier than George's, but Duncan supposed that was because a servant could not risk being inelegant in elevated company. Duncan felt a kind of swell of pride watching his employee behave so properly. Had Davies always been that way? If anything, Duncan would have counted Davies as highly *in*formal. But perhaps that was Duncan's own fault for encouraging a friendliness between them that crossed the usual lines drawn between master and manservant.

Even the word "master" made Duncan uncomfortable.

"How ever did you find this place?" Richard asked abruptly, his thundercloud gaze on Davies.

Yet George was the one to answer. "A fellow in town pointed us in this direction."

Richard transferred his attention to the man beside him. "What town?"

"Birchmere," George told him. "Fitzbert, by the way. George Fitzbert. And that," he pointed with his fork, "is Davies, but he's secretly a lord."

Edward stopped watching whatever Odette was designing

with her sorrel and swung his head to look over at Davies. "Are you?"

"No," said Davies.

"Come off it, Davies, no need to hide it," George said.

"Lord of what?" Richard asked.

"Montcliffe," answered George. "What are the odds we'd be down here just when——"

"I am not Lord Montcliffe, nor do I have any intention of being Lord Montcliffe," said Davies.

"Could you be? If you wanted?" Adelia asked.

Duncan had never seen his valet angry, and he suspected that anyone who didn't know Davies well would not perceive the atypical tightness of his voice, the rigid grip of his hands on his cutlery. George, as per his nature, seemed to be baiting Davies for his own amusement. Duncan made a mental note to give George a thorough rebuke later. At that moment, all he could do was to try and soften things to avoid a scene. But before he managed to find a way to verbally part the two men, Richard said, "Quite high, actually."

A pause rippled around the table as everyone tried to place his words in a context. Finally, George asked, "What?"

"You asked about the odds. They are quite high, since a lord is just what we require."

"What——? How——?" But George seemed unable to find an appropriate entrance into his question.

"Faebourne has a way of providing what we need," Adelia explained. "Despite my mother's attempts to the contrary."

"And you need a lord?" Duncan asked. "To go with the song?"

Adelia's smile wavered. "The blood of one. And a few other things as well."

George leaned forward to look down the table at her. "Blood?"

"Not all of it!" Edward said then looked apprehensively at his brother. "Right?"

"Well, how much of it then?" George demanded.

"I'm not a lord," Davies said quietly but firmly.

George huffed. "His mother was Lady Georgiana Lyming, the only child of the current Lord Montcliffe."

"And she was disowned, and I have no plans to seek his title," Davies said.

Duncan attempted to process this new information. "Why, Davies," he said, "you outrank me!"

Davies slapped his palms on the table, and everyone jumped where they sat. "Unless you need me, *sir*, I would like to be excused."

"Oh, don't be like that," George cajoled.

But Davies kept his unflinching gaze on his employer, and Duncan, confused by the turn of events, felt he did not have the authority to deny him. "Of course," he said.

Davies pushed away from the table, stood, gave the tiniest of bows, and strode out of the dining room while the rest of them watched in silence.

CHAPTER 23

*D*espite his irritation, Davies took care in removing the borrowed garments, gently returning them to the back of the chair so that he could brush and clean them later. He found his bag waiting at the foot of his bed, and he dressed in nightclothes with the hope of putting the whole provoking day behind him. Sleep would do him good, and on the morrow he and Duncan and (if only there were a way around it) George would puzzle out a way to fit themselves in the curricle and go home. Maybe the Milnes would allow him and Duncan use of their carriage—it was the least they could do after abducting his employer—and George could travel back alone.

It was a satisfying notion, one that allowed Davies to relax against his pillow. He didn't particularly worry about the Milnes wanting his blood; as he wasn't a lord, he did not qualify for—

Davies sat up abruptly. At the time, he had been so diverted by all the other oddities and George's vexatious goading that the idea of people seeking the blood of anyone, peerage or no, had failed to perturb him. But considering it now, it was quite alarming. He'd grown up with the stories, after all. Blood was for witches and dark magic.

His gaze traveled to the ceiling, where the dying fire left wavering shadows that, in Davies' current state of mind, looked like demons.

They needed to leave. Soon.

Not because Davies honestly thought the Milnes would bleed him—he still firmly considered himself beyond their stated requirements, nor would Duncan allow it... he hoped. But if this eccentric family were caught up in the occult he wanted no part of it.

Davies threw back the bedclothes then hesitated. He needed a plan of action. Dress, pack, gather George and Duncan... Perhaps steal the carriage?

He had his nightshirt half over his head when a knock sounded at the hallway door. "Davies?" George's voice was muffled by the thick wood. "I know you're in there. If you don't open this door, I'll..." A pause as, Davies assumed, George tried to come up with a suitable consequence. "I'll start calling you 'Lord Montcliffe' whether you like it or not."

Davies hastily pulled the nightshirt back on and grabbed his dressing gown for good measure.

"Well, then, Lord Montcliffe it is!" George said, and the door rattled near the bottom; Davies guessed George had kicked it.

Some low muttering was followed by Duncan's voice. "Never mind him, Davies. May we come in?"

Davies pulled open the door, revealing Duncan and George standing, well, not quite shoulder to shoulder as George was a bit taller. "I was just about to get dressed," he informed them.

George pushed past him into the room and with an apologetic grimace, Duncan followed. "Dressed? Why?" George asked.

"We can't stay," said Davies. He glanced out into the empty corridor, half expecting to spy a flame-colored eavesdropper. Nothing. He sighed with relief and closed the door. "In case you hadn't noticed, these people are planning some kind of blood ritual."

"With your blood, no less," added George.

Davies' brows lifted. "And whose fault is that?"

"Gentlemen, please," said Duncan. "Though, Davies, I have to say I am quite put out that you never mentioned your family connections. If I'd known—"

"I didn't discover it myself," Davies told him, "until two days ago, when you disappeared."

Duncan blinked at him. "I've only been gone a day."

Davies exchanged a swift, confused glance with George. "No," George said, drawing the world in a long, low lament, "it took us a day to discover the whereabouts of Faebourne, and we left the following morning. *This* morning."

"This is my first night here," Duncan insisted. When Davies and George shook their heads in tandem, he grabbed his already untidy dark curls with both hands. "How is this possible?"

"This place isn't right," said George.

Duncan began to march to and fro before the dying fire, a habit Davies recognized as born from irritation. And as usual, George was the reason for it. How many times had Davies stood and patiently listened to his employer complain about something George had said or done? Davies snuck a look at George, but the man was remarkably unself-aware. He watched Duncan as though his friend were some kind of entertainment. Though Davies thought he spied a crease between George's brows. Might it be concern? It seemed impossible that George Fitzbert has such feelings.

Having walked off some of his head of steam, Duncan stopped and rounded on his companions. "It's strange, I'll grant you that," he said. "But it's not a bad place, and the Milnes are not bad people!" He drew a deep breath and continued more calmly, "They need my help. *Our* help." He went on to explain the curse and his quest.

The line between George's brows deepened and Davies felt his own forehead tighten as he tried to make sense of what he heard.

"They're not out to hurt anyone," Duncan insisted. "They only abducted me out of desperation." His face fell. "After all, given more time and options, I'm sure they'd have chosen just about anyone else." With a rueful look at Davies, he added, "And maybe it's you they need more than me."

"That's what I'm afraid of," said George, and Davies' heart skittered a bit. What reason did George have to be fret over *him*? They'd come for Duncan, after all. *Duncan* was George's friend, not him, though for some reason reminding himself of this pained Davies. He felt as though he'd lost something at the same moment he told himself he'd never had it to begin with.

"I'm less worried for my own sake," Davies said. "I'm not convinced I meet their criteria for the blood of a lord. But we shouldn't linger." He frowned around at the room. "There is bewitchment here."

"That's you being superstitious as usual," said Duncan.

"You've just lost a day!" George cried.

Duncan's frown deepened. "Which means their fortnight would be a month in London."

"Assuming the difference in time remains consistent," said Davies. "In many stories, if one does not escape immediately, one never escapes at all. We must go, and soon, else we risk being stranded here permanently."

But Duncan shook his head. "I promised. I may not be much in the world, but I am a man of my word."

For a long moment the three men simply stood there, staring at one another. Exhaustion ached in Davies' bones, and all at once he wished the others would go away so he could sleep. They could tackle the problem again once they were all refreshed and thinking clearly. Then George turned to him and said, "Well, *you* can't stay."

Davies' heart jumped again, adrenaline washing the fatigue away, and he studied George's face in an attempt to understand. *Does he actually care? Or does he just want me gone?* But George's expression was guarded, unreadable save the fierceness in his amber-colored eyes.

"I didn't come all this way just to turn around and run home," Davies told him. "Not without Mr. Oliver.

"Oh," he went on, remembering. He crossed to where his bag rested on a hassock at the foot of the bed and withdrew a stack of clothing which he presented to Duncan. "It's only enough for a couple of days, I'm afraid. I didn't anticipate a stay."

Duncan accepted the neatly folded pile with an indulgent smile and a glance down at his person. "Well, but they've given us clothes. Nice ones, in fact."

Davies smiled and eyed his employer's now wrinkled and

askew cravat. "And you seem to have done just fine without a valet."

"In spite of the lack, not because of it," Duncan assured him. "Though if you really are Lord Montcliffe's grandson—"

"Don't you start, too," Davies warned. "Oh! I almost forgot. I couldn't fit your boots in, but..." He reached into his bag once more and extracted a pair of black leather shoes.

Duncan threw back his head and laughed.

CHAPTER 24

*A*fter Duncan had assured Davies that he did not need help getting ready for bed and returned to his room, George remained. Not only remained but showed no inclination to leave. Davies stood staring at him—had George forgotten this was not his room?—and George merely stared back.

At length, George asked, "You're sure it's all right for you to stay?"

Davies attempted to smother the smile that rose to his lips. "In my own room?"

The humor did not take; George's expression continued to be grave. "At Faebourne."

His sobriety was infectious, and Davies' levity plummeted. "We'll soon find out. As I said, I'm not convinced I'm any use to them."

"I don't share your conviction," George admitted, "but even if I did, and even if you're right—do *they* know your blood won't work?"

Davies privately hoped the theory would not be tested.

Abruptly, George went to the door that connected their chambers. "Journeys end and all that," he said, and Davies could hear the forced mirth in his tone, the way his words caught in his throat, could see even in the dim of the dying fire the tightness around his eyes.

"Best get some rest," Davies agreed. But his exhaustion notwithstanding, it was a long time before he slept.

~

DAVIES' world jogged around him—even though his eyes were shut, he felt it, the rapid back-and-forth of his head rocking on his pillow. Then he heard someone say his name: "Davies!"

Reluctantly, he opened his eyes. The rocking ceased, but a hand remained on his shoulder. Not his own hand. Davies' gaze tracked up the arm to find George standing over him.

"I've figured it out!" George said, far too loudly for so early in the morning.

"Very happy for you, Fitzbert," Davies mumbled. He closed his eyes and turned his face back toward his pillow.

"No, no, no, no," George said. Davies felt the mattress dip as George sat down. "Wake up! This is important!"

Davies sighed. He'd only known George a couple of days, but that short acquaintance had already proved George would not let go of an idea once it seized him. Resigned, Davies rolled onto his back and opened his eyes again, blinking as his face met sunlight. George must have opened the drapes.

"Hm," George murmured. "The Montcliffe line is handsome indeed."

Davies rolled his eyes and sat up, suddenly keen to put some distance between himself and his companion. He slipped off the far side of the bed and stood up. "I'm sure that's not what you came in here to announce."

George's mouth—and it was a generous mouth, Davies noticed somewhat unwillingly—twisted with contrition. "No," he admitted. "But it seemed worth saying anyway." He brightened then and sat up straighter. "Listen! The Milnes need the blood of a lord—"

"Don't—" Davies began.

George waved the pending protest aside. "Montcliffe is ill, possibly dying. Isn't that what the fellow in town said?"

"Percy Harding," Davies recalled, suspicion crawling up his

arms and spine with unpleasantly cold fingers. "Yes, I believe he mentioned something of the sort. Why?"

"He's a lord," said George. "He has blood. That he probably won't need much longer."

"Dear God," said Davies. "Are you suggesting we kidnap a sick old man—a man who may be dying—and bleed him to death?"

"Well, when you put it that way, it sounds awful. But I'd really rather him than you. He disowned your mother for marrying someone she loved. I'm not sure he deserves our sympathy."

"I'll speak for my own sympathy, if you don't mind," Davies said.

George grimaced and became suddenly intrigued with a loose thread on the bed clothes. He pulled experimentally at it as he said quietly, "Not to death, anyway."

"Pardon?" Davies asked.

"We don't know that it's to death, do we? The bleeding? Duncan doesn't seem to think so," said George.

"In which case, it might as well be me."

George looked up, and Davies didn't much like the sly smile hovering around his lips. "Ah, but you were so sure your blood wouldn't suit."

Davies huffed, irritated at being cornered. "Why does it matter to you whether the Milnes get blood or whatever else they need?"

"The sooner they're satisfied, the sooner we can get Duncan home," said George, and this time Davies could see the real worry on his face, the lines there thrown into contrast by the morning sun. "I don't think this place is good for him. Or you."

His concern caused Davies' throat to tighten. He coughed discreetly so as to get his words out. "Never mind me. It's Mr. Oliver who needs rescuing, and if to do that we have to help him finish his..." He flapped a hand. "Quest or whatever, then I suppose we'd better prepare ourselves to do just that."

"Strap on our armor, so to speak?"

"Yes, well, our clothes will have to do. Speaking of which," Davies moved to gather the discarded garments from the night before, "bring me yours." At the sight of George's lifted eyebrows, Davies said, "I'm a valet. Someone needs to care for them."

George stood up and bowed. "Yes, Lord Valet."

"I'm not—"

"A lord. I know," said George. "You're too good to be a lord. More like an angel." And with that he all but skipped off to his own room, leaving Davies standing alone and nonplussed.

CHAPTER 25

*D*uncan went down to breakfast wearing his own clothes —which, much to his personal satisfaction, he'd managed to put on without seeking out Davies for aid—and shoes. He discovered Richard and Edward already seated at the table, as well as a slightly altered Odette: the red in her hair had become more pronounced, her nose had straightened, and her face rounded with a less pointed chin. Edward had evidently not lost any interest in her, and while he chatted—more *at* Odette than *to* or *with* her—Richard sat across from them and glowered. Though when Duncan entered the dining room, the black look changed direction to strike him instead.

Duncan took it in stride; he had come to understand Richard's constant irritation should not be taken as personal, nor was Richard meant to be feared. He was somewhat like an old dog that growled its displeasure at the world around it because it had no real power to change its circumstances. Framed thusly, Duncan felt rather sorry for Richard Milne.

But as Duncan moved to take a seat beside Richard, his host's brooding shifted to surprise and what Duncan thought might be distaste. "You go there," Richard informed him, pointing at the head of the table. "Surely you know this by now?"

Exasperated and not a little offended, Duncan asked, "Why?"

When Richard only stared, he went on, "Well, who sits there when I'm not here?"

Richard stared some more and Edward, diverted, said, "No one."

"But it should be you," Duncan told Richard. "As head of the family. That's the proper way."

"None of us can sit there," Edward said. He rose from his chair and Richard said, "Edward," in a sharp tone of warning. Unheeding, Edward went around to the head of the table and reached for the chair.

The chair caught fire.

"Oh!" said Duncan, jumping back a step. He scanned the table wildly for a pitcher of water, a cup, any kind of liquid that might extinguish the blaze.

"It's all right," said Edward. "See?" He released the chair and the flames subsided. "They never burn anything. Not even the wood."

Indeed, the chair appeared unharmed.

"Still not very comfortable to sit in," Edward went on.

"You've tried?" Duncan asked, astounded.

Edward shrugged. "A few times, just to..." He glanced at his brother and did not finish his thought.

"In truth, I was surprised when the chair accepted you," Richard told Duncan.

"You thought you would put me in a burning chair?!"

"He didn't think you were the right one," Edward said with a small smile.

"Edward!" Richard barked, his voice like a thunderclap. Even dreamy-eyed Odette started and looked around, torn from whatever reverie she'd been inhabiting.

For the first time since meeting him, Duncan saw Edward appear sullen. "Do you still have doubts? He can sit in the chair! What more proof do you need?"

Before Richard could respond, a voice from the doorway said, "The Seat Perilous."

Duncan turned; Davies stood near the far end of the table, a thoughtful frown on his face. "I suppose it's perilous for the wrong person," Duncan agreed.

Davies chuckled. "This is where my mother's love of old stories comes in handy. The Seat Perilous—or Siege Perilous in some versions—was a chair at the Round Table that was deadly to any but the knight worthy to find the Holy Grail." He lifted his eyebrows at his employer. "Which appears to be you, sir."

"Not *deadly*, though," said Duncan. He looked to Edward. "You've sat in it."

"Mummy didn't want us to hurt us," Edward said, and his gaze wandered to Odette, who had gone back to daydreaming as she hummed softly to herself.

"She didn't want us to succeed either," said Richard, eyeing Duncan. "Else she would have chosen someone with more fortitude."

"Or wouldn't have cursed Adelia in the first place," added Edward, his attention still on the oblivious Odette.

As though summoned by the sound of her name, Adelia materialized behind Davies. "Mummy didn't choose Mr. Oliver," she said. "Aloysius did."

Ever the gentleman, Davies stepped aside and drew a chair out for the lady. Duncan privately scolded himself for not doing it first, particularly when he saw the warm smile with which she rewarded the valet as she sat down. *He's the help and yet his manners are better than mine. Well, but he was raised by the daughter of an earl, and my mother died when I was twelve. How could I possibly compete?*

Aloud, Duncan said, "Maybe Davies here would be a better choice."

Three startled faces greeted his words—Odette did not acknowledge them at all, and Richard turned instead to examine Davies.

"You know about quests and chairs and things," Duncan told his valet. "You're even named for a knight, aren't you?"

"Oh, but Aloysius chose you!" Adelia cried.

"Still, your chances might be better..." Richard said thoughtfully.

"Aloysius is never wrong," Adelia insisted.

Duncan's gaze met Davies' and he could tell his man was trying to read him, to understand his motivations. Did he truly believe Davies should step in? Or was he simply worried about failing and seeking an escape to keep from losing face? Even Duncan didn't know the answers, but something bitter was spreading over his tongue, and he felt sure it might be envy. Which seemed preposterous, to be jealous of one's valet, but Davies was handsome and refined and so damned confident. Not in the showy way of George, but in the reserved way of someone who truly trusted himself and his abilities and had no need to prove or demonstrate them.

Davies cleared his throat and said, "A quest once begun must be seen through to the end, sir. However, I'm happy to serve as your squire, or in whatever capacity you'd find most useful."

He even makes eloquent speeches, damn him. But Duncan recognized the gesture as one meant to cast him as the hero... And also let him know he wasn't alone.

Adelia clapped her hands together and beamed as though every pale fiber of her being produced light. "Yes! Exactly!" She turned her shining eyes to Davies, and that sour taste flooded Duncan's mouth again. "And you, my lord, will surely have a part to play."

Duncan watched Davies narrowly for his response to being addressed as "my lord," but Davies was too polite to object. He merely smiled and inclined his head before taking a seat himself.

It took a moment for Duncan to realize he was the only one left standing. Not only that, but everyone was looking at him, even Odette, whose thoughts had apparently wandered back to the present moment. Duncan inched his way toward the chair at the head of the table the way a man might move toward a dog that has been known to bite. The chair, however, failed to ignite or do anything else un-chairlike, and deciding the stares were worse than potentially being set aflame, Duncan finally sat down.

Almost immediately, footmen sprang (as, Duncan was learning, was the habit at Faebourne) seemingly from nowhere and began serving breakfast to the newcomers. Duncan found the thin, lightly toasted and buttered bread to be above standard, and he wondered again about the practically invisible staff. Aside from the footmen, including the glassy-eyed man with the tea cart the day before, he had not seen any sign of a housekeeper, cook, butler, or other such servants. A house so large as

Faebourne surely required many hands to keep it tidy. So where were all those hands? Had they been instructed to keep from view? Yet the Milnes did not give Duncan the impression they were harsh employers. Simply... eccentric. Perhaps their unpredictability caused the staff to avoid them?

As he nibbled and mused, Duncan became aware of Odette's gaze on him. He looked over to see her biting her lip as she studied him. "I am sorry, Miss Odette," he said. "I am not much of a breakfast companion, am I?"

Her tiny white teeth released the lip and she smiled. "I am not used to breakfast. Or companions. So I don't really know." Her smile melted slightly. "It's difficult to stay a person here," she said. She glanced over at Edward, whose eyes were wide as he listened intently. "If not for you," she said, "I'd have evaporated already."

"Evaporated?" Edward asked, eyes going round with alarm.

"When many people are around, I can't always form one solid image." She looked again to Duncan. "You all think of so many different things, and different people, and I can't..." She shook her head then smiled once more at Edward. "But your feelings are so strong, and the picture in your mind is very clear. That gives me something to cling to and makes me able to stay."

Duncan observed the way their eyes met and reflected again on the possibility he was witnessing two people falling in love. Except one of them wasn't a person.

"We need the cauldron back," Richard said, cutting into Duncan's thoughts.

Duncan turned to him and nodded. "The grass shoes are upstairs."

Davies set down his tea and pushed his chair back from the table. "I'll fetch them for you, sir."

But Duncan held up a hand to stay him. "Eat first. I suppose Fitzbert is sleeping late. Always was a night owl."

"Actually," Davies began, but then halted as his cheekbones turned pink. Beside him, Adelia smiled then threw a knowing look at Duncan, though whatever she knew, Duncan didn't. Mostly he wished Adelia would stop smiling at his valet.

"Actually?" Duncan prompted.

"He was awake rather early," Davies finished. "Though he may have gone back to sleep. Our rooms connect," he added for clarification. He looked apprehensively at Adelia. "He had some odd ideas about ways to help you, but I think you had best tell us what you need first."

"A song," Duncan said, with a gesture at Odette. "And your cauldron, which I'll recover. And..." His hand moved from Odette to Davies, but he couldn't bring himself to say it aloud.

Adelia saved him the trouble. "The blood of a lord, yes." That dazzling smile, once again aimed at Davies, though he didn't appear to appreciate it. He merely cleared his throat and said, "I'm not technically a lord, however."

"You're of noble blood," Richard said. "It will do."

Davies' temper visibly slipped. "Oh, I'm so glad to hear it has your approval," he snapped, causing Richard to rear back where he sat.

"Just, er, how much blood are we talking about?" Duncan asked.

Adelia and Richard exchanged glances that Duncan could not decipher. Richard said, "We need the knife as well."

Davies blanched.

Adelia nodded thoughtfully. "And the fairy mirror."

"Not anything we can exactly nip into town for," said Duncan.

"Who's nipping into town?" George asked as he sailed in looking somehow stylish and disheveled simultaneously. He dropped into the chair next to Davies and put a hand out as though he might touch the valet's face or else take his hand, but then his fingers closed, a fist grasping air, though the movement seemed to require concentration and effort. As if the hand had been acting on subconscious orders and George had only narrowly stopped himself.

Davies saw it, too; Duncan noticed the way Davies' eyes tracked the motion of George's hand the way one watched a bee in fear of it stinging.

Still, none of the cheer left George's face or voice as he said, "Are we going for Montcliffe after all?"

"Montcliffe?" Duncan echoed.

George threw Davies a reproachful look. "Didn't you tell them?" To the rest of the gathering, he said, "We worked it out—"

"Not we," Davies murmured.

"Montcliffe is a lord, isn't he?" George continued. "More of one than Davies here. No offense, Davies. In any case, he's a crotchety old man that no one likes or will miss, and he's close to dying anyway—"

"We don't know that," Davies interjected.

George smiled broadly at him, and Duncan wondered how it was *everyone* seemed to smile at Davies all the time. Had it always been that way? Or was it only now that everyone knew Davies came from titled gentry that he became suddenly worth the extra attention?

Duncan frowned at his own thoughts, the envy twisting in his stomach. It was unbecoming, and unlike him. He valued Davies, not only as a good employee but a friend and confidant, someone knowledgeable whose level head (and extensive network of domestic intelligence—it occurred to him that George and Davies shared a love of gossip) had saved Duncan more than once from social embarrassment.

To Davies, George said, "Well, then, we shall just have to go find out."

Davies' dark eyes met George's amber-colored ones, and Duncan could almost see the battle occurring between them. "We are *not* abducting an old man," Davies finally said in a tone that suggested he'd said it before.

Multicolored eyes wide and eager, Edward said, "Oh, but it's not that difficult!"

Davies turned on him, brows low. "It's not a question of difficult. It's a question of propriety. Abduction is not only illegal, it's ungentlemanly."

If Edward—or any of the Milnes—caught the underlying censure in Davies' words, they failed to show it.

"But what if," George suggested, "we could actually help him?"

Six faces swung his way, five of them hopeful and attentive, and one skeptical and suspicious.

"How?" Davies demanded.

"I don't know," George admitted, undeterred by details. "We can't know until we see him for ourselves."

Another long moment passed during which Davies and George held another silent and invisible duel. Then Davies turned to Duncan and said, "It's your quest, sir. How should we proceed?"

Duncan looked at the gathering around the table, and a tiny bit of pride swelled in him. Yes, he was the one it all fell to. For once, he had consequence.

Also, Adelia was smiling at him—*him*—those pale blue eyes shining with absolute trust. He could not fail her.

"It's worth a look at least," Duncan decided. "You go and see Montcliffe. I will fetch the cauldron, and then we can gather whatever else is on the list."

CHAPTER 26

"I'll just get your shoes before we leave," Davies told Duncan as the party exited the dining room. He glanced at George, who was already making for the main door, no doubt off to get the curricle ready. "Who knows when we'll be back," he added, "what with the time differences and all."

"You may be in need of some special shoes yourselves," Duncan said. "It seems the—the house, or the grounds, or the trees... I don't know what, really, but *something* prevents people from leaving if it thinks those people are helping Miss Milne's cause."

"And the grass slippers trick whatever it is?" Davies asked. Duncan had mentioned it the night before during his explanation of the circumstances at Faebourne, but it sounded no more sane in daylight. Then again, nothing about their current situation seemed sane. It felt more like the old romances filled with knights performing impossible tasks in order to save stranded damsels.

His mother would have been delighted.

At the thought of her, Davies saw her. Not in his mind's eye, but in life, standing in the entry hall. He turned to stare.

His mother had been tall and slender, with a pointed, pale face and honey-colored hair that fell in long waves when she left it down. How he'd loved to watch her brush it. She'd looked very like the illustrations in the books she'd relished—like a princess, waiting at the window for her beloved hero's return. Alas, Davies' father had ceased returning when Davies was only four. The dragon sea had won.

And yet his mother had continued to sit at the window. The difference had been that, instead of expectant vigilance, she'd sat with a book instead, for as long as the daylight slanted in to illuminate the pages. Sometimes Davies sat with her, and she would read those stories to him.

The woman in the entry was not Lady Georgiana Lyming. Davies knew because, despite looking exactly like her, she walked entirely differently. His mother had stepped lightly, as though not wanting to leave any marks on the world. She'd hardly seemed to take up space. The woman in the entry, while not ungraceful, came across as more confident, and a degree less kind.

The woman looked at him, and her smile was wrong, too. Davies' mother had smiled wistfully, tentatively. This woman smiled knowingly. Cunningly.

A shiver ran down Davies' back.

He must have stared too long because Duncan turned to look. "Oh," he said, "she's changed again."

"Who?"

"Miss Odette. She was the one beside Edward Milne at breakfast."

Davies tried to recall, but the woman had been quiet and left no impression on him. "She is the song you spoke of?"

"Yes," said Duncan.

"I don't—" Davies began, but then he heard it. "A harp?" he asked. His mother had played the harp.

Duncan shook his head. "It's different for everyone, I think."

"What do you hear?"

Duncan paused to listen then grimaced. "Sounds rather like opera to me."

Davies well knew that Duncan did not enjoy the opera. "I thought you were meant to hear songs you like."

"Songs that stay with you," said a musical voice at Davies' shoulder. He drew away in surprise. Odette smiled at him, that same slow yet sharp smile, like a blade moving slowly over some-one's throat. "For good or ill."

If Duncan perceived anything dangerous in her, he did not show it. "What's this, Miss Odette?" he asked, gesturing to her changed appearance.

She dimpled at him. "Ask Mr. Davies."

Duncan's brilliantly green eyes turned to the valet, and Davies said to Odette, "You look very much like my mother, ma'am."

"If so, then it is only because you have a very clear memory of her," said Odette.

Davies said nothing. He *had* been thinking about his mother, after all.

Then Duncan said, "Perhaps... Perhaps Miss Odette could accompany you to Montcliffe. Her abilities may be useful in smoothing the way?"

It was the last thing Davies wanted, but Odette beamed. "I could try!"

"Try what?" Edward drifted over. His gaze swept Odette and a shadow disappointment crossed his features. "You look different."

"Songs have similarities," she said. "They use the same notes. But they don't all sound alike."

It didn't sound to Davies like a direct answer to Edward Milnes' observation, but Edward seemed to take it as such. He nodded gravely, as though her words had been profound.

"His song was louder," Odette went on with a glance at Davies. "But now..." The gold began to fade from her hair, and she shrank a little, becoming less willowy and more petite.

Davies stepped away from her and from the group they'd formed in the entry. "Your shoes," he said to Duncan and fled up the stairs. He wasn't sure what about Odette distressed him; no one else appeared to suspect her of anything sinister. *The whole situation is just so strange*, he told himself. *I'm surely suffering some kind of hysteria induced by disorientation.*

At the top of the stairs he hesitated, realizing he did not know in which room Duncan had been installed.

A flash of orange near his left ankle nearly caused him to trip.

Aloysius traipsed ahead and stopped by a door. "Is this the one?" Davies asked him. He pushed open the door and sighed.

Duncan Oliver was not an untidy man, exactly, but something of an absent-minded one. Clothing tended to be discarded haphazardly as though Duncan forgot about his garments the moment he shed them. Therefore, it took Davies a few minutes to hunt down one grass slipper (under a chair) then the other (across the room near the wardrobe).

So gathered, Davies prepared to bring them to his employer, only to nearly run directly into Miss Milne as he exited the room. She stopped walking, her mouth falling open at the sight of him.

"Miss Milne," he said when it became clear she might just stand and stare at him indefinitely. Aloysius, he noted, had made himself scarce.

The gape of her mouth became a dazzling smile. "Mr. Davies!" She made it sound as though she were ecstatic to see him. Then her gaze fell on the shoes in his hands and her jaw slackened once more.

"Mr. Oliver needs them," Davies said. "To fetch the cauldron. Isn't that so?"

"Oh. Yes," said Adelia.

"And will we?"

"We?"

"Mr. Fitzbert and I. Will we need them in order to leave?"

Adelia looked at the shoes again, head cocked as if suddenly bewildered by them. "There is only one pair," she said.

"Ah," said Davies, mostly because he was not sure what else to say.

"The curse only obstructs my champion," Adelia said, then stopped to consider. "And Faebourne likewise attempts to keep out anyone or anything it sees as a threat. The two are rather at odds, really. In any case, I do not believe you will require grass slippers. If anything, given your position in being able to help my cause, the curse almost certainly would rather you be gone."

I might rather be gone, too, Davies thought, his mind spinning as he tried to weave together all the raveling threads that made up the larger tapestry of their circumstances. But it was impossible;

they could only continue and do their best to see it through to its end. So he smiled and offered Adelia his free arm, shoes hooked by the fingers of his other hand. "We'll do what we can to help," he promised.

As they descended the stairs together he thought he spied an irritated expression on Duncan's face, and he definitely did catch one on George's. By the time they joined them in the entry hall, however, both men had smiles affixed.

"Your shoes, sir," Davies said.

Duncan frowned. "I'm not sure you should continue to call me that."

Davies returned the frown. "Why is that?"

"Well, you outrank me."

Davies suppressed a groan. He felt like he would never live this family connection down. Perhaps confronting Montcliffe was the best option after all. Only then would he be able to put his life back in order.

To Duncan, he said, "I have no rank. Sir."

"Not officially, anyway," George chimed in. "But we'll set things straight, won't we? What's this?" he added when Odette abruptly appeared at his side. She stood there, trembling, a mish-mash of features: blonde hair streaked with auburn, blotchy skin, one green eye and one brown.

She grabbed hold of the sleeve of George's jacket and looked up at him, swaying where she stood. "I must get away," she said. "There are too many thoughts here. I feel as though I'm being torn apart!"

A cascade of discordant notes filtered into Davies' consciousness. He only just stopped himself from clapping his hands over his ears. From the expressions on the others' faces, they were suffering similar discomfort.

"If she disappears," said Duncan, "I don't know that we'll be able to catch her again."

"This is why you should have used the cauldron!" Richard snapped from the doorway of the Small Room. Davies wondered how long he'd been there. Something about Richard Milne—his grey, stonelike personage—caused him to blend in with the shadows around him and allowed him to lurk, invisible, until he wished to be seen or heard.

"I will go fetch it," Duncan promised, going so far as to step out of his shoes and into the slippers. To George he said, "Take her with you."

"There's barely room for two of us!" George protested.

"Take our carriage," Adelia said.

George looked at Davies, who shrugged. His good breeding —and he *was* well bred despite his objections and a childhood and employment that suggested otherwise—did not permit him to voice his true opinion: that he did not like Odette and did not want her anywhere near him.

Still, the lady's expression made it clear her distress was genuine. Davies' shrug became a nod, and George took Odette's hand and wrapped it around his arm. "Let's get the carriage," he said. "Some fresh air will do you good, eh?"

Odette looked up, her gaze pinned to George's face as though her very existence depended on her focus. And perhaps it did; Davies still did not entirely understand how any of it worked—Faebourne, the Milnes, or this strange woman Duncan said was a song in human form. But as Odette stared at George, she began to change. All her mismatched parts started to resolve themselves into something cohesive and familiar.

Too familiar.

The dark hair (had it become as shaggy as that? he would ask Mrs. Bentham for a trim as soon as they were home), the dark eyes, the posture so correct it showed that he did not have the leisure to slouch... On Odette's new form, Davies' very waistcoat mirrored back at him, down to the one loose button that needed to be resewn.

George shook Odette's arm off and stepped away from her. Or him. "Out," he said hoarsely.

Davies wondered if he appeared as bewildered as Odette did at George's word. She—Davies had to think of her that way; he couldn't think of her as himself—only continued to look up at George, her brow furrowed.

"Go wait outside!" George roared, and everyone in the entry

recoiled. But, Davies realized, the cacophony had ceased. Something low, slow, and mournful had taken its place.

With a small sob, Odette flung herself out the front door. George squared his shoulders and, without looking back, followed.

The remainder of the party stood staring at Davies. He looked to Duncan. "If that will be all, sir..."

"Yes, Davies, I believe that is all."

"We'll be back as soon as we can be," Davies assured him.

"It will seem longer to you than to me, I think," Duncan said.

It already feels like we've been here an eternity, thought Davies.

With a slight bow to his employer, and another to Miss Milne, he left.

CHAPTER 27

The path was much more agreeable in daylight. Not that Duncan had found it particularly *dis*agreeable the evening before, but with the sun's aid, he felt more self-confident in being able to see where he was going.

Said sun only intermittently pierced the canopy above, creating dappled ripples of light on the ground below. If at night the path glowed with seeming starlight, by day it winked like sunlight on the crests of waves.

Well, if those waves were dirt.

Poet you are not, Duncan told himself. He wished he could remember how far along the bench had been, but time and distance did not behave naturally at Faebourne and its environs.

On his feet, the grass slippers crackled now and again. The grass used to make them had begun to dry out, making it more friable. Duncan hoped the shoes would last long enough to get him back to Faebourne, if not long enough to see him through any additional tasks.

He trudged onward, grateful for the shade and the slight breeze that managed to twine its way through the trees. The day was uncommonly warm for April, and he could feel the perspiration threatening to break out across his brow and nape, could hear the dull thud of his own heartbeat in his ears. *I should have brought a hamper like last night*, he thought, *or at least a jar of lemon-ade*. He could only hope he'd find the bench and cauldron soon.

His steps slowed. The heat shrouded him like a physical thing, weighing him down and fatiguing him. He wandered onward, only half aware of his surroundings.

Suddenly, a spark of light flashed from the ground, piercing Duncan's gaze and jolting him to full alertness. He squinted, trying to pinpoint the source. But a fresh gust of air moved the branches above him and the light winked out.

Yet another yard along the path, a second light glittered.

And farther along still, a third.

Could this be what had caused the path to glow the night before? No, Duncan decided, a few shiny... what, stones?... wouldn't be enough to cause such illumination. But he could not overcome his curiosity. Halting, he waited. The branches swayed as the air circulated through them.

There!

Duncan dove before he could lose sight of it then nearly cut himself when he snatched it out of the dirt: a piece of broken glass. And not just glass, he realized as a portion of his own nose reflected back at him. It was a bit of mirror.

Foreboding flooded Duncan's heart. Hadn't Adelia said they needed a mirror? A fairy mirror, as he recalled.

He pocketed the fragment and waited for the trees to move again. So going, little by little he gathered the splinters, having all but forgotten the cauldron he'd originally set out to fetch. He didn't know if there were a way to piece the mirror back together—and perhaps it wasn't the fairy mirror at all—but he felt compelled to collect the shards all the same.

He had no inkling of how long he'd been following the trail of glass when a sweet scent tickled his nose and drew his attention away from his self-imposed task. Looking up, Duncan beheld the largest wild cherry tree he had ever laid eyes on. Indeed, he'd had no idea they could grow to such height or girth. It would have taken three, maybe four men with hands clasped to encircle the trunk. And of all the trees around him, it was the only one in bloom. Its white, cup-like flowers made it a bride of the forest.

Not only did the tree bloom, but vines of climbing flowers that Duncan could not identify—blues and whites and some purpley pink—embraced the cherry's trunk like a lover. The perfume from all these blossoms made Duncan's head feel light. The sight was beautiful but the smell nigh on nauseating.

Above him, the trees sighed in the wind, and two more fragments signaled their positions in the dirt. Duncan hurried to add them to his growing collection. *How big is this mirror?* he wondered. It seemed to him fairies made things on either a very small scale or a very large one. He had enough pieces of glass now to know this mirror did not fall into the former category.

As he picked up the second of the two shards, which lay near the cherry's roots, Duncan noticed a hollow in the tree trunk. At first he thought it merely a small hole; the crowd of vines and fall of flowers hung nearly to the forest floor, and the cavity only showed below the curtain of creepers. But upon closer inspection, the opening proved large enough for a man to stoop into. A petite woman could have walked in upright.

Not inclined to venture into strange trees, Duncan almost bypassed the hollow to continue on his way. But as he turned away, something caught his eye.

For one thing, the interior of the tree was not dark, which seemed odd, though not as odd as much of what Duncan had witnessed in the past day. He supposed his tolerance for the extraordinary had increased due to near constant exposure. In any case, he could see through the straggling vines into the hollow, and it seemed to him someone had painted the inside of the tree. It was a soft aquamarine color, and a jewel-colored rug and a number of large tuffets covered the ground. All of that would have been enough to garner interest, but the thing that caught Duncan's eye was the cauldron.

It squatted on a tree stump that appeared to be a kind of low table. As with the mirror fragments, Duncan could not positively identify it as the Milnes' cauldron, but it seemed to him the likelihood of more than one small iron pot in the woods was slim. Then again, if someone were living in the tree—and it looked to him very like someone was—perhaps he or she *would* have a small cauldron to cook with. If so, Duncan did not want to steal it from him. Or her.

"Anyone here?" Duncan asked. Though he could see the small space was unoccupied, it felt polite to inquire. When no answer came, he glanced around outside to verify the resident was not, in fact, lurking about nearby. The forest remained as empty as ever.

He deliberated over his options. He could continue searching for the bench from the night before and see if the cauldron was still there. He could wait by the tree for whoever lived in it. He could go in, uninvited, and wait, though propriety advised against it. Or he could simply go in and take the cauldron. Propriety most certainly advised against *that*.

He had just decided to keep walking and perhaps return to the tree later when something else in the tree caught his attention.

A mirror.

Or what was left of one.

It lay face-up on the patterned rug, its ornately carved wooden frame blending into the carpet's swirling design. Round and large as a tea tray; Duncan might even have mistaken it for one if not for the remaining silvered glass that clung to the edges of the wood like broken teeth. He would have missed seeing it altogether but somehow, despite the lack of sunlight in the tree, the mirror had beckoned him with a flash akin to the winking of its brethren on the forest path.

He needed the mirror.

He needed the cauldron.

There they were.

Or something very like them. But Duncan felt more and more certain that, yes, these were the objects the Milnes required. Richard himself had said that Faebourne strove to provide for their needs.

Glancing around again to confirm he truly was alone, Duncan ducked through the opening in the tree. Inside, he discovered he could stand without trouble so long as he removed his hat, which, as a gentleman, he did upon entering. He lingered near the threshold, uncomfortable with his own intrusion. But urgency drove him onward. *Perhaps I could leave a note...*

Alas, a scan of the quarters revealed neither paper nor quill and ink. Indeed, the premises were quite spare: rug, tuffets that Duncan presumed acted as both seating and bedding, the smaller tree stump upon which the cauldron sat, the mirror discarded on the rug, and a lantern that hung above. It had no flame per se— that surely would have been dangerous inside a tree—but a glowing orb inside it that looked as diffuse as dandelion down. Duncan studied it, trying to understand how it worked, but he could not make sense of it.

One more oddity, and not one of import, he decided. He still felt guilty about taking the items, but he could not think of a way to leave an explanation that would excuse him. *There is no excuse for stealing*, he told himself. But if the cauldron, at least, belonged to the Milnes, then someone had taken it and he was only reclaiming it.

As for the mirror, based on its condition Duncan concluded it was not valued and perhaps not wanted at all. In which case the occupant of the tree would not be sorry to have it removed.

He knew he was rationalizing, but doing so was the only way he could bring himself to act. That, and recalling Adelia Milne's hopeful expression when he'd agreed to help her. A proper knight would not hesitate to do whatever necessary to champion his lady.

Not that Adelia was *his*. Of course she wasn't. And many a legendary knight courted his chosen lady from afar. Not that he was *courting* Adelia. Of course he wasn't.

Head spinning with these thoughts, Duncan stepped further into the hollow. It was about as far as he could go; another step and his nose would have met the back wall. If "wall" was the correct word for the interior bark of a tree.

He reached down for the mirror and a dilemma arose. He required one arm to hold his beaver hat. The mirror most certainly required two hands. And then there was the cauldron to consider.

No other thing for it: he had to put on his hat. As he did so, it knocked the lantern above his head. The fixture swung and smacked his hat right back off again.

With a sigh, Duncan reached up and stopped the lantern's motion. Then he bent to retrieve his hat, careful to step sideways from under the light before placing it on his head. He then lifted the mirror to test its weight. The wood was solid and heavy; he would need both hands to carry it back to Faebourne.

He eyed the cauldron. Too burdensome to carry on his arm for any length of time. Perhaps he could carry it on the mirror? Not on the glass side—what was left of it—but on the back?

He turned the mirror over and set it down, then centered the cauldron on the smooth, walnut-colored wood of the reverse side. Then he lifted the mirror once more, carrying the cauldron with it. Yes, very like a kettle on a tea tray. Only much heavier. Not an ideal construct, but it would have to do.

Keeping low so as not to upset the lantern again, Duncan scuttled out of the tree. A small rain of petals fell after him as he pushed through the vines of climbing flowers. Straightening, he looked around a final time, unsure whether he hoped someone would be there so he could ask proper permission for the relics, or whether he dreaded being caught and having to explain himself. It hardly mattered, however, as no one materialized to either blame or absolve him.

With a deep breath—one that nearly caused him to choke on the overwhelming perfume of the blooms around him—Duncan turned his steps back toward Faebourne. The mirror and cauldron were heavy in his hands, but as he contemplated his victory (and the approval in Miss Milne's eyes) his steps were lively just the same.

CHAPTER 28

George drove, of course, which left Davies to sit in the carriage with Odette. To his relief, she no longer looked like him, but to his consternation, she'd gone back to looking a bit like his mother. Not so much as before, but Davies recognized aspects of his mother in Odette's frame and face. Lady Georgiana's sharp, high cheekbones and honey hair were in evidence. Odette's eyes, however, were amber. His mother's had been indigo.

Trying not to be too aware of Odette's attention, which based on her stare was very focused on him, Davies watched out the carriage window as the trees rolled past. As Adelia Milne had predicted, the topiary had not shown any belligerence nor prevented them from leaving. He wondered whether Duncan might have suffered some misconception... Though, if so, it meant the Milnes had either induced the hallucinations somehow, or else they shared the delusion. And—Davies sneaked a glance at the woman across from him—there was certainly no simple explanation for Odette.

Unless he also was being humbugged somehow? And George as well? Something in the food perhaps?

"Blast it," Davies muttered. Every time he thought he'd made progress, he found himself back at the start.

"I beg pardon, Miss Odette," he added. "I should not speak

in such a fashion with a lady present." Not at all, if his mother had been correct. Davies could not recall whether his seafaring father had sworn but it seemed unlikely. Something about Lady Georgiana Lyming kept one from wanting to sully themselves in her presence.

Of course, Odette was *not* Lady Georgiana Lyming. She looked less like his mother every minute. Her hair retracted as though drawn back into her skull and turned from honey gold to burnished bronze. "I needn't be a lady," she said, and her voice had grown deeper, too.

"Stop that," said Davies.

"Then you must stop thinking about him," she admonished.

"I'm not thinking about anyone." He returned his attention to the window and concentrated on the fresh, unfurling spring foliage.

"I cannot turn into a tree," Odette told him. "And if I do not stay in human form, I will disappear."

"Must you take your form from my thoughts?" Davies asked, genuinely curious. "How does it work, being a song?"

"Songs often make humans think of those they love... or despise... Sometimes both feelings apply to one person," she said with a rueful smile. "As a song—as a collection of songs, rather— I am..." She sought the word. "*Bent* by the thoughts of those who hear me."

"But I do not hear anything," said Davies. "There is no song to make me think of my mother or..." He waved a hand at her current form. Mostly George, though too narrow in the face. Even as he thought it, Odette's face broadened to fit his mental image.

"People sometimes remember wrong," she said. "And, no, you won't always hear me. But I'm there, like a childhood memory that comes abruptly to mind and then lingers."

He eyed her. Something about her words sounded more like a threat than a promise to him, and though she looked as innocent as she could given she wore George's likeness, Davies all too clearly remembered her cunning smile from earlier.

If she suspected his misgivings, she did not show it. Instead, her attention turned to the carriage window. "Oh!" she said.

The trees had thinned and the Birchmere church came into view.

"Have you ever been in a town before?" Davies asked.

She gave her head a tiny shake, never taking her eyes from the window. "Look at all the people," she breathed. "The buildings..."

"You should see London," said Davies. Then a thought occurred to him. "But if so many people at Faebourne made it trying for you, won't a town be far more difficult?"

Finally, Odette returned her attention to him. "I hadn't thought of that. Please—" She startled him by reaching over and placing her hand on his. George's hand. Despite their gloves, the intimacy both thrilled and confused him, and his mind began to fog. "Think of someone," she pleaded. "Concentrate!"

Disconcerted, Davies discovered that thinking of someone upon command was a nigh impossible thing to do. If anything, it caused his mind to go blank.

"Someone! Anyone!" Odette said, squeezing his hand.

"You know people," he countered. "Why don't you think of someone?"

"That's not how it—"

If she said more, Davies did not hear it, could not over the sudden noise of a discordant orchestra. It played so loudly, he turned to look for it as though it might somehow be in the carriage with them. Then he realized: it was Odette, of course. He turned back to her, but the skirts of her dress were fading.

"I can't," she said. "I can't hold a form."

The Milnes believe they need her for some reason. Duncan believes he needs her to fulfill his quest. I will not be the one to lose her.

But she was half gone already, the bottom half of her dress a mere mist, and still that cacophony blazed through his head like a hot brand. Her hand on his began to lose substance; he no longer felt the weight of it.

Davies closed his eyes and picked out a thread of the music in his mind. Not his mother's harp, yet it was familiar somehow. He followed the sound and the rest fell away. A pianoforte, played by fleet, white hands.

"Who was he?"

Davies opened his eyes, and the young man sat across from him, a small smile on his face. The blond hair that fell in natural ringlets to his shoulders, the almost ridiculous amount of lace at his throat and cuffs. He'd been as pretty as a girl and had all but dressed like one, too.

Davies cleared his throat. "Someone I knew but briefly."

"He made quite an impression, it would seem."

"Not really," Davies said, striving to sound unperturbed despite the lump forming in his throat. "I hadn't thought of him in years. But the pianoforte... One of his passions."

"*One* of his passions." Her smile broadened, knowing. When Davies did not respond, she went on, "As I mentioned, memories are often buried in music."

The coach turned past the church, and Davies focused once again on the view outside the window. Like the day before, few people walked the streets of Birchmere; it did not appear to be a popular destination, or even a regular stop for travelers. No wonder he and George had garnered such attention.

Well, that and the fact he ostensibly bore a strong resemblance to Lord Montcliffe. Perhaps meeting the old man—assuming they even got so far; it was just as likely they would be turned away—would give him a glimpse of his future. He'd see what he might look like in old age.

The carriage began to dip down the hill but then came to a halt. George's words carried to where they sat: "Mr. Harding!"

Percy Harding's voice followed. "Returning so soon? But where is Lo— Er..."

"Davies," George supplied. "He's riding indoors today."

Holding his hat on with one hand, Davies obligingly tipped his head out the open window. "Good morning, Mr. Harding."

"Oh!" said Percy, lighting up at the sight of him. "Are you going to Montcliffe after all?"

Davies grimaced. "We are. But," he added before Percy could read too much into it, "then we must return to Faebourne."

"You found it?" Percy asked.

"It wasn't difficult," said George.

"No one I know has ever found it," Percy told him.

"How many have gone looking?" George asked.

Percy's mouth opened, closed, opened—this time accompanied by a raised finger, as though there were a point to be made —then closed once more. The finger, however, remained poised, a visual exclamation mark.

"Well, then," George said, thereby ending the discussion. Davies felt the carriage shift as George resumed the reins. "Since you seem to stroll here daily, perhaps we'll see you again on the way back." And with that, they began to move.

Davies pulled his head back in, and Percy tipped his hat at him as they passed.

"Why are you so set against it?"

The words, coming from the figure of someone he'd known so long ago, momentarily confused Davies. "Against what?"

"Becoming Lord Montcliffe."

Was he imagining the judgemental expression? Wynn had often looked at him like that. He would have asked the same question, too. Wynn had never let Davies forget the difference in their stations in life, though Davies conjectured he'd come off better as a valet than Wynn must have done as a priest. He'd been, after all, a third son—coddled, yes, and wealthy and refined, but with no expectation of ever inheriting.

"You knew your mother was a lady," the false Wynn across from him went on. "Yet you did not pursue the connection? You did not seek to find your lost kin?"

"An apple does not reattach itself to the tree." His mother had always said that whenever Davies expressed curiosity about her family.

"It doesn't fall far from it, either."

Davies eyed him—her—with suspicion. "And what tree did you fall from?"

"A cherry tree," she said, and the answer was so breezily absurd, so like Wynn, as to be uncanny.

"Hm." He turned back to the window without further comment, felt the coach dip down the hill then rise again on what, he realized, had to be the road that led to Montcliffe. Some minutes later they rolled to a halt. As Davies moved to open the carriage door, he heard George say, "I'm not a coachman!"

The carriage door swung away from Davies' fingers, revealing a tall footman in saffron livery trimmed in gold. He let down the step. Meanwhile, George continued to shout, "Davies! Tell them I'm not a servant!"

Davies gestured for Odette-as-Wynn to precede him, and she stepped out of the carriage. George's tirade changed to, "Who the devil are you? Davies!"

With a deep breath, Davies straightened his shoulders and tried to remember everything his mother had taught him.

He descended from the carriage ready to confront his heretofore obscure past.

CHAPTER 29

*D*uncan returned looking more bedraggled than he felt proper, but carrying the mirror and cauldron had put him in a lather—of the literal sort. With his hands occupied, he had no opportunity to straighten his clothes or make himself even passingly presentable. Indeed, he could not even open the door, though it proved unnecessary; as he came to the veranda, the door opened and a furry, orange head came around the jamb.

"How the devil did you do that?" Duncan asked.

The door opened further, revealing Adelia Milne, her smile wide and warm in a way that sent tendrils of pleasure down Duncan's back. "Aloysius said you'd returned."

"Did he?" Duncan asked with another glance at the fox, though brief, for he preferred to absorb Adelia's happy expression. "You seem to be the only one he talks to."

At this, Aloysius sat and gave Duncan a hard stare that communicated quite effectively. "Or not," Duncan amended, and Adelia laughed. The tendrils extended from Duncan's back down into his very toes.

"That looks heavy," she said, reaching to take the cauldron.

"No, quite all right," Duncan assured her. "If you will just hold the door open and tell me where..." He eased past her into the house only to run directly into Richard, who took possession of the items in Duncan's hands without consultation. Nor did

Duncan have the strength to cling to them; he released the mirror and cauldron without protest.

Richard turned and stalked into the depths of Faebourne but Duncan hesitated. Should he follow? Or go and freshen himself up?

Adelia surprised him by coming up beside him and taking his arm. "Oh," he told her, "I really should..." He used his free hand to remove his hat. Adelia looked up, and her lips quirked with amusement. Yet she said, "I assure you, Mr. Oliver, you are perfectly presentable."

He very much doubted her veracity but found himself reluctant to remove from her company. So he allowed her to lead him to the Small Room. There Richard and Edward waited, the cauldron having been parted from the mirror, which had been turned upright, each item sitting on the table in the center of the room.

Without prelude, Richard pointed at the mirror and demanded, "Where did you get this?"

His tone put Duncan's back up, making the response stiff. "I found it. With the cauldron. In a tree. As I recall, a mirror was one of the things you said you need."

Adelia said, "Yes."

At the same time, Richard said, "It's broken."

And Edward asked, "In a tree?"

"I have more of it," said Duncan, choosing to address Richard's complaint first. "I found all these bits of it along the path." He reached into his pockets and extracted the collection of slivers, dropping them onto the wood of the mirror. "I'm not sure if I found all of it," he admitted.

"A mirror works no matter how many pieces it is in," said Adelia.

Richard pursed his lips. "True."

"In a tree?" Edward asked.

"I thought, perhaps, given the odd circumstances, it might be a fairy mirror," said Duncan.

"Only one way to find out," said Adelia. She stepped to the mantel and picked up a small silver bell Duncan had never noticed. It gave a dainty tinkling sound when she rang it, and almost immediately Aloysius appeared in the doorway.

"Will this mirror do?" she asked.

Aloysius trotted over to the table, reared up, and put his forepaws on it for a better view. Ears forward in an attitude of interest, he turned his head one way then the other. Duncan would almost have believed the creature was admiring himself in the remaining intact pieces of glass.

After a minute, Aloysius sat back down and looked up at Adelia. She brought her hands together and beamed. "Yes!" she declared, and Duncan let out a long, relieved breath.

"Then only the knife remains?" he asked.

"Assuming your friends return, and the song with them," Richard said. His dour tone indicated skepticism.

"They will," Duncan vowed. "And now, if you will excuse me, I believe I require fresh clothes."

"And I will see that luncheon is ready when you return," Adelia declared. "You must be hungry after such a morning."

Duncan gave her a small bow, even as his stomach agreed with the lady's assessment. As he exited the Small Room, eager to wash and make himself neat, he heard Edward one more time: "In a tree?"

CHAPTER 30

The footman only betrayed his surprise by widening his eyes slightly at the sight of Davies. His expression remained neutral as he gestured them up to the house. *More like a castle*, Davies thought. The place had to be at least two hundred years old... or designed to look it. Despite the weathered stone, which had faded to a golden color in the sunlight, it appeared chilly. Davies shivered, though he told himself it was simply due to stepping into the shadow of the portico.

A sharp-eyed butler waited at the door, and he evinced no more astonishment than had the footman as Davies and his companions entered the hall. There, he took George's and Davies' hats—pausing uncertainly before Odette and her lack of hat—and all their coats and gloves. Then he silently led them to into a square parlour dominated by tall windows.

"Did they want a drawing room or a solarium?" George muttered as the butler withdrew.

Davies watched the servant go. "They didn't ask our names. Or for a card, not as I have one."

"It's pretty clear who you are, I think," said George. "You, on the other hand—" He pointed at Odette.

She widened her blue eyes innocently and looked to Davies.

"An old..." He paused, uncertain of his next word. "Acquaintance."

George eyed him. "That you think about, evidently, if she's turned into him."

"Not *into*," Odette protested mildly. "I don't become the person. I only look like them."

"Splitting hairs," said George, his gaze never leaving Davies.

"The situation was rather more complicated than me simply thinking about an old friend," said Davies.

"I thought he was an acquaintance," George said.

Davies' temper began to slip its leash. "What difference does it make?"

George snorted and turned away, wandering in the direction of the front windows.

Davies looked at Odette. "Do you mind possibly changing your appearance?" he asked.

"You'll need to think about someone else," she said.

Davies glanced at George's stiff, straight back but swiftly decided against that direction. Changing Odette into any other form at this point would surely alert an observant staff. She had to remain as Wynn for the time being, whatever George's personal fury—which, in any case, Davies did not understand. After all, it was *his* past being plundered and thrown in his face, not George's. First Wynn, now Montcliffe. Davies' hands fisted at his sides as he quashed his irritation.

The parlour door opened again, and the butler reappeared. A craggy fellow, tall and shrewd looking; possibly once a military man, given his bearing. He bowed and said, "Lord Montcliffe will see you now."

Davies opened his mouth to demand how Lord Montcliffe could even know who they were, but George caught his eye and gave a tiny shake of his head. So all Davies said was, "Thank you."

As the butler led them upstairs, he said, "Lord Montcliffe is not always... clear about who or what is going on around him. Please try not to agitate him."

Ah, so perhaps it didn't matter who they were. But Davies resented the implication that they would knowingly upset the man.

They climbed one flight of stairs then another. At the top of the house the rooms became taller and larger, the windows letting in even more light. They stood in the long gallery for a moment, the butler clearly proud of the view. Birchmere nestled below, but despite being able to see for miles, Davies could not pinpoint Faebourne's location. Past the Birchmere church, he saw only a sea of treetops. Of Faebourne's gothic roofline there was no sign.

After a minute or two of quiet admiration, the butler wordlessly turned and continued to a door at the far end of the gallery. It was tucked into a corner and papered to match the walls so as to be nigh invisible. The butler tapped twice, lightly, and opened the door before any answer could be made. With a low bow, he announced, "Lord Montcliffe, your guests have arrived." Then he stepped aside to allow Davies, George, and Odette into the room, closing the door behind him as he exited.

The chamber was filled with light from the tall windows and papered in a soothing shade of blue. In a darker blue brocade chair beside one window sat an older gentleman, impeccably dressed. His fine, white hair lay thin across his scalp, his skin only a shade or two darker. Eyes the same deep blue as Davies' mother's regarded them. They appeared sharp enough to Davies, whatever the butler had said.

"So," Montcliffe said, "you are my grandson."

Davies gave a neck bow of acknowledgement.

Montcliffe's gaze wandered to George and Odette. "And these are?"

"Mr. George Fitzbert and, er..." Davies frowned at Odette, unsure how to introduce her. He half hoped she might speak for herself. Her attention, however, was riveted to Lord Montcliffe. As she stared at him, her golden hair slowly lengthened, and she grew taller where she stood.

Montcliffe made a strangled noise that startled Davies. He poised to jump to the old man's aid, but Montcliffe seemed unharmed aside from his evident shock at the sight of Odette. Davies opened his mouth to attempt an explanation, but then Montcliffe croaked, "Georgiana."

Davies looked again at Odette, and yes, she had taken the form of his mother. Not quite as he remembered her—this version appeared younger, more spirited than the soft but sad woman he'd grown up with. But the features were unmistakable.

Odette smiled and stepped forward to take Montcliffe's outstretched hand. "Papa," she said, her tone musical but huskier than Georgiana's had been. Yet it must have been long enough since Montcliffe had heard his daughter speak, for he did not question it. Nor did he ask how Georgiana could still be so young. Tears were in his eyes, welling and unshed, as he gazed at Odette.

Feeling forgotten—worse, like a voyeur—Davies looked to George, who shrugged.

Odette leaned over Montcliffe, and he released her hand and put both his hands to her cheeks. "My girl." His voice was hoarse. "My beautiful girl. I should never have... You got my letters?" he asked suddenly. "Yes, you must have. It's why you're here, isn't it?"

She gently pulled away. "And I've brought your grandson to meet you."

Montcliffe tore his gaze from her with obvious reluctance, recentering his attention on Davies. "No question he's a Lyming, eh?" he asked as he peered at his grandson.

Davies did not entirely understand everyone's certainty. He did not consider himself to look like his mother, and he did not see himself reflected in this man's visage either. His skepticism must have shown because Montcliffe clucked. "I didn't always look old and frail. And," he said raising his voice, "I'm not nearly as half-dead as my staff wants to believe!" He paused, then laughed wheezily. "He's out there, you know. Listening. Ready to spread gossip." His smile became a scowl, and he pushed himself up out of his chair on shaky legs.

Without thought, Davies moved to help him stand but was batted away for his efforts. "None of that," Montcliffe said gruffly, even as he wobbled and listed. "Come. Let me show you the proud line from which you descend. Your father's people may have been nobodies—"

"Papa," Odette said warningly, and Davies' brows lifted in surprise at her audacity.

Montcliffe sighed. "Yes, well, it's all in the past," he said, though he still sounded aggrieved. "One didn't marry for love in my day, you know. And how was I to know he wasn't angling for the money?"

"Papa!"

"I never honestly thought you'd go." His voice cracked and he appeared close to tears again. "It's been so long..." Then he straightened his shoulders and rallied as best he could given his shuffling walk. "This way," he directed, "though your mother must know where it is."

"I hardly spent my time staring at the family portraits," Odette answered primly.

Montcliffe harrumphed. "True enough. Could hardly get you indoors at all."

The statement felt like a slap to Davies; the mother he'd known had spent all her time indoors reading and drifting from room to room like a ghost. To have it so plainly suggested that she had not always been thus—that she had been, possibly, someone else entirely—shook him at his core.

The old man led them to the door, which George leapt forward to open. Montcliffe paused and scrutinized him. "Friend of the family, are you?"

George smiled thinly. "I like to think so."

"And what do *they* think?" Montcliffe asked.

George's eyes met Davies'. "He is," Davies decided. "Quite a good friend, in fact."

Montcliffe harrumphed again and proceeded out into the long gallery. If the butler had been lurking as the old man accused, he'd since retreated. "Everyone always looks at the windows," Montcliffe said. "They never turn around to look at the wall."

Davies bit back a gasp at the series of portraits hanging along the back wall of the gallery. From more than a few of them, versions of his own face stared back. Not exact, but indisputable. His chin, his eyes (shape, not color), his dark hair (his mother had been the cuckoo in the nest in that regard), his smallish ears, his slightly sloping shoulders—all were evident in the parade of his ancestors.

George stated the obvious: "Well, you're definitely one of them."

"I am sorry, Georgiana," Montcliffe said as they gazed at the portrait nearest his bedroom door. It featured what Davies took to be the current Lord Montcliffe only much younger. A rectangle of discolored wall beside it suggested the absence of one of the paintings. "I took yours down after…" He stopped and shook his head. "Not out of anger but because it broke my heart to see you every day."

"You could have reconciled at any time," George said, and Davies gaped at him. "If it made you so sad, why didn't you go to —" He stopped and glanced at Davies. "Wherever and make things right?"

Montcliffe turned to Odette. "But you received my letters! You must have! I tried for so long to coax you home. After I heard that… *he'd* died… I even sent money!"

Understanding began to resolve in Davies' mind. "Only after my father died were you willing to forgive her, is that right?"

"That man left you with nothing!" Montcliffe insisted. To Odette he said, "You could have come home, maybe found a proper match. Raised your boy in his family home. What took you so long to come back?"

"We heard you were ill," said Odette. "We did not want to next hear you'd passed on without having made peace."

Montcliffe eyed her for a long moment. "I see," he finally said, his tone having gone from plaintive to cold. "All too well, in fact. You came to claim your inheritance, eh? Before I could hand it down to my nephew. *He's* been visiting during my 'illness' as so many insist on calling it. The ingratiating little brat." This last came out as a mutter. "It's more than I can say for you." He turned his hawkish gaze on Davies. "Either of you."

"To be fair, Davies here didn't know he was related to you until a couple days ago," said George.

Montcliffe drew back and studied Davies a moment longer. Then he turned back to Odette. "Is this true? You never told him?"

To her credit, she appeared suitably chastised. "I did not. I didn't want him thinking about what he didn't have, or might have had... I didn't want him to hate me for the choices I'd made."

Davies swallowed a lump that had unexpectedly formed in his throat. Had that possibly been the reason his mother never said anything? His grandfather had sent letters, and she never once mentioned them or him.

"I don't want it, anyway," he said. "This house or your title. I wouldn't know what to do with any of it."

"Good," Montcliffe said, and Davies blinked at him with surprise. He couldn't decide whether he felt relieved that Montcliffe would not press him on the issue, or offended that his grandfather didn't try harder to change his mind. But then Montcliffe went on, "The only people who should have titles and wealth are those who don't want it. Makes you a damn sight better choice than Nash.

"I'll have Mrs. Talbot make up your rooms," he went on, turning toward the door at the far end of the gallery. It was the one the butler had showed them through, the one that led to the stairs, and the walk seemed impossibly long for the old man.

To prevent him going to the trouble, Davies said, "We can't stay."

Montcliffe rounded, frowning, brows lowered.

"We are staying with friends. They will be waiting for us," Davies explained. "We will be back..." He gave an uncertain grimace in Odette's direction. "*I* will be back."

Montcliffe hesitated, then nodded. "Yes, well, don't make it too long. We have much catching up to do and I'm running out of years."

"Are you..." George began, and Davies was surprised by the gentleness of his tone. "Are you truly ill?"

"If age is an illness, then I've got a terminal case," Montcliffe said. "Nash keeps telling the town I'm on my deathbed. Does it so the people of Birchmere will bow and scrape at him." He coughed a laugh. "He's never been my heir, you know. He made an assumption, and I did not correct him." He looked to Odette. "When you sent me word that I had a grandson, I made sure he would inherit. Not his fault I'm a fool." He turned back to Davies. "Let's hope that bit isn't in the bloodlines.

"Now," he continued, "As this is the most excitement I've had in years, I'd best go rest." He began to make his slow way back toward his bedroom, paused and said again, "Don't wait too long to come back."

Odette flashed a conspiratorial smile at Davies then hurried to Montcliffe's side. "Let me help you, Papa."

Montcliffe gave a dismissive wave but did not protest when Odette took his arm.

Davies and George watched their progress, and once they were inside the chamber with the door closed, George said, "I wonder what she's planning."

"Maybe she's just being kind," Davies suggested, though the sense of foreboding he'd experienced before concerning Odette continued to flow through him.

"It's a put on," said George.

Stunned by George's corroboration of his own feelings, Davies asked, "How can you tell?"

"Known enough schemers in my day." He flashed a smile. "Been one myself a time or two."

"Is that a confession?"

"Haven't anything to confess at the moment."

"Keep it that way," said Davies, and though he meant it lightly, George's expression—just for a second—appeared hurt. But it disappeared so quickly Davies could not be certain he saw it at all.

The bedroom door opened again, and Odette slipped out, an uncharacteristic grin on her face. Which was to say, Lady Georgiana's face. *Mother never smiled like that*, Davies thought. *Not like someone who'd just pulled a prank.* Because his mother would never have done such a thing. At least, not as he'd known her. Who knew what she'd been like before? The visit to Montcliffe had given Davies an idea of the unplumbed depths of his late mother's character. He'd always thought he knew her best, but now it seemed he'd never truly know her completely.

"I got it," Odette said as she hurried up to them.

"Got what?" asked Davies.

"The blood."

He and George stared. Finally, George said, "You bled him? Just now?"

She nodded, still grinning, pleased as someone who'd won a wager.

Davies and George exchanged glances. "Is he all right?" Davies asked.

"He'll be fine," Odette assured them. "But we should probably go."

"Is he likely to raise a hue and cry?" asked George.

"He's asleep," said Odette. "And unlikely to remember anything once he wakes. But still and all..."

"Yes," Davies said. "Sooner gone, sooner done with Faebourne and all this."

"Not all *this*," George countered, his open palm sweeping to encompass the gallery. "But I daresay Duncan will need a new valet."

Davies did not respond, merely turned and made for the far door before pausing and looking back. "You," he said to Odette, "had best change back into Wynn."

"Think of him," she said.

Davies closed his eyes and conjured the image. A minute later he opened his eyes to find Wynn standing beside a scowling George.

"*Who* is Wynn, exactly?" George asked.

"No one important," said Davies. "Come, let's get back to Faebourne and see this whole mess ended."

CHAPTER 31

George froze when Davies climbed up beside him on the carriage seat. "What are you doing?"

"I can't ride back with her," said Davies. "You said yourself she can't be trusted."

"Trust me, then, do you?" George asked.

"Given the choices."

"Rather a snug ride for two."

"Good thing we're both thin," Davies observed.

George made a noncommittal noise and set Thunder and Storm to motion. Now and then Davies swayed against him, their shoulders brushing. Davies didn't appear to notice. George tried to ignore it by making small talk.

"Does this mean you're a viscount now?" he asked.

"What?" Davies had evidently been woolgathering. "I don't know. I don't want it."

"Want it or not, it's yours," George told him. "Hm. Montcliffe's other titles... Henry would know."

As they cut through Birchmere, the few people out and about stopped to watch them pass. "I should have ridden inside after all," said Davies. He closed his eyes briefly.

"What are you doing?" George asked.

"Concentrating. Don't you hear the music?"

George tried to listen, but the horses required too much of his attention. "No," he finally admitted.

"We just need to make sure she doesn't disappear before we get through town," Davies told him. "She very nearly did the first time we passed through."

George took that as an instruction to speed up, at least until the church fell behind them. Once he felt it was safe to slow down, he asked, "What will you tell Duncan?"

"I don't know," Davies admitted. "First things first. We must do this ritual and get Mr. Oliver home."

"No use in you going back to London, though, is there?" The idea set a gloom over George. Not seeing Davies... Not that he'd have any reason to see him even if they were both in London. One didn't spend time with their friends' valets. "Never worry. I'll see him home safe."

"Maybe you'll get an invitation to Dove Hill," Davies remarked.

George lifted a brow. "Do you think so?"

"Well, you're certainly welcome to visit Montcliffe."

Their gazes snagged. George quickly unfastened his to focus on the horses again.

They said nothing else for a long while.

"Does it seem like the sun is coming up?"

Davies' voice after so long a silence startled George. Truth be told, he'd been in too deep a study to notice, but now Davies mentioned it... "It was afternoon when we left Montcliffe."

"Yes," Davies confirmed. "It should be getting darker now, not lighter."

Yet the farther they drove, the earlier it appeared to be, so that by the time they arrived at Faebourne, the sun hung directly overhead.

"Time really is strange here," said George wonderingly.

"The whole place is strange," said Davies. "I think the less time we spend here, the better."

"Agreed." The carriage rolled to a stop and a groom appeared from seemingly nowhere, his face a blank as George tossed him the reins. An equally vacant-looking footman unfolded the step for Odette as George and Davies climbed down.

"Staff doesn't seem quite right, either," George murmured to Davies as they made their way up to the house. "Haven't seen a butler or housekeeper..."

Even as he said it, the front door swung open to reveal not a butler or other servant but a fox. Aloysius looked up at them and almost appeared to smile. Then he looked past them and put his ears back.

George turned. The groom had disappeared with the carriage and the footman with him, but Odette remained standing in the drive.

"Aren't you coming?" George asked.

She—still in the guise of Davies' mysterious friend Wynn—smiled ruefully. "I cannot without the shoes."

"Shoes?" George echoed.

"I believe she means the grass slippers," said Davies. "I will go see if Duncan has returned." He slipped past Aloysius and disappeared into the house.

George met the fox's gaze. "You don't like her either?"

Aloysius' attention returned to the stranded song as Davies re-emerged with the slippers. They looked, in George's opinion, rather the worse for wear. "He's back, then, I take it," George said.

"Only just," said Davies as he walked by to place the shoes before Odette. "He was freshening up for luncheon. We should consider doing the same."

A streak of orange flew past George then. It grabbed one of the shoes in its teeth and darted away.

"What—?" Davies stammered.

"Why, that little..." said George, though with a quantity of admiration in his tone.

Neither man moved to pursue the fox. Davies turned to Odette and said, "I'm not sure what's gotten into him."

"No matter," she said. "If you will simply allow me to place my hands on your shoulders?"

George watched narrowly as Davies, clearly too gentlemanly to decline the request, gave a small nod of permission. Odette took off one of her shoes and slipped the foot into the remaining grass slipper. Then, holding to Davies' shoulders, she hopped on one foot from the drive onto the front path.

"There," she said, "hardly any trouble at all." Showing no sign of releasing his shoulders, she looked Davies in the eye. George didn't much like her expression, something sinister and knowing, as though they shared a dark secret. He couldn't see Davies' face to judge the valet's response to this, but it took a fair amount of effort on George's part not to go force the two of them apart.

He made a mental note to ask Henry about anyone named Wynn.

Davies stepped back, out from under Odette's grasp, and bent to retrieve her discarded shoe. "Hardly," he agreed, handing it to her.

Adelia came hurrying out of the house just then, a partially shredded grass slipper in her hand. "Oh! I've just wrested this from Aloysius!" she panted.

"It's all right," George told her. "We made do with the one." He nodded toward where Odette was exchanging the borrowed shoe for her proper one.

"I can't think what came over him," sighed Adelia.

"Only feeling lively, I'm sure," said George, though he suspected otherwise. Aloysius had the same misgivings about Odette as he and Davies. Yet the fox had been the only one willing to take action. *Damn our good manners. Serve us right if they end up doing us in.*

"No harm done," Odette said as she and Davies came up the walk. George eyed Davies, trying to determine whether her words were accurate. Davies rewarded him with a half smile that failed to belie his discomfort. Whoever Wynn was, his presence —even in false form—appeared to distress Davies. And Odette seemed to know and enjoy it.

Only one thing to do. George aimed his gaze at Odette's shoulder blades and thought, clearly and with all his might, of Thomas Gulliver. Gully was a short but muscular Irishman with oily ginger hair and a large moustache who only just got by on the side of respectability due to having a number of wealthy men in debt to him. In his mind, George heard the rise and fall of a cheerful jig.

Odette must have sensed his intention, for she turned to look over her shoulder, even as that shoulder fell several inches into her compact new frame. George smirked back. "Sorry," he said, with no true hint of apology in his voice, "just remembered someone I'd promised to visit. Guess it will have to wait."

Without comment, Odette turned around again and marched into the house. Davies blinked after her, his expression clearing like a man whose worries have lifted.

"Let's go wash up, shall we?" George suggested, falling into step beside the valet as they entered the house. "I could do with some lunch."

CHAPTER 32

*D*uncan ticked the items off on his fingers. "Cauldron, song, mirror, blood..." This last came with a small frown in Odette's direction. She once again had the long, reddish-gold hair and feminine form of who he assumed to be the late Mrs. Milne, but he also detected the faint leavings of a ginger moustache over her lip.

"We only need the knife," said Adelia from his other side.

They sat at the table, the remains of bread, cheese, and fresh fruit littering their plates. Only Odette's dish remained full; she idly nudged a gooseberry across it with a fingertip.

"Do you know where it is?" Duncan asked. The thought of yet another walk in the woods exhausted him.

"Mummy kept it," said Edward, his eyes on Odette.

"Oh!" Duncan said. "Well, that saves us some trouble."

"Not really," said Richard. "We don't know *where* she kept it."

"It's a family heirloom," Adelia explained. "She wouldn't have thrown it out, but she didn't want us to use it, either."

"So she hid it," George deduced.

They stared at one another until, at length, Edward said, "I suppose we'll just have to look for it."

"What does it look like?" Davies asked.

"It's silver," said Adelia.

"One solid piece of silver," Richard clarified, "handle to blade."

"And the handle is carved," Edward added, "rather like the mirror you found."

Odette's head swung up at that. "Mirror?"

Clearly pleased to have won her attention, Edward smiled broadly and said, "Found it in a tree of all things."

"I did say mirror," Duncan said. "When I was listing everything. I'm sure I did."

"I'm sorry," Odette told him. "I wasn't attending."

"Is it very large?" George asked.

Duncan looked down the table at him. "The mirror?"

"The knife."

"Ah." Duncan turned to Adelia, brows lifted as though to re-communicate the question.

"We haven't seen it in years," she said. "Not since we were young. It looked frightfully big to me then."

"It's not, really," said Richard. He held each of his index fingers some seven or eight inches apart in the air to indicate the size.

"Mummy used to say it was made from the moon," Edward said with a grin that invited Odette to share his amusement. She stared blankly at him.

"Moon*light*," Richard corrected.

"Where did you last see it?" asked Duncan.

The Milne siblings exchanged a flurry of glances. "Her sitting room?" Adelia replied, though she didn't sound certain.

Richard shook his head. "That would be too simple."

"I saw it once in the library," said Edward.

"There's a library?" Duncan asked, momentarily distracted by the fact that a room existed that he had yet to see. He supposed he shouldn't have been surprised; Faebourne was large, and he'd not seen nearly all of it. Though he had seen every room on the ground level, which, in his experience, was where a library would most usually be found.

"Upstairs," said Richard, as though answering Duncan's thought. "Mother said the light was better for reading there."

Upon reflection, Duncan was inclined to agree. The trees

crowding the downstairs windows would make a library situated there too dim to be useful. Unless one wished to waste candles or oil.

"Well then," said George, pushing back from the table, "we should split up and begin searching."

Edward continued to beam at Odette. "Will you help me look?" he asked her.

Her blank expression lasted a moment longer before she blinked and smiled. "Of course."

"Miss Milne," Duncan said, "I'd most appreciate your guidance. I'm sure I'd get lost otherwise."

"Certainly," she said. She turned to Richard. "How shall we divide the house?"

"Edward, you and..." Richard gestured at Odette but seemed for some reason unable or unwilling to name her. "Should check the library, since you remember seeing the knife there." He was, Duncan thought, quite in his element when giving orders. "Adelia, take Mr. Oliver through the chambers in the East Wing. I'll manage the West Wing." He looked over at George. "You and Mr. Davies can search the rooms on this floor."

Thus instructed, the party disassembled. Duncan and Adelia followed Edward and Odette up the stairs. But when the other two continued down the main hall, Adelia turned right.

"Oh," said Duncan, "this is the wing my room is in."

She nodded. "There are a number of rooms to examine, I'm afraid."

"Are they all as big as mine?"

"Sometimes." She stopped in front of the first door and pushed it open, revealing a room bedecked entirely in cranberry-colored brocade with gold trim save the deep green rug and decorative wall papers. It felt dark despite the large window opposite the door.

"I much prefer mine, I think," Duncan said as they stepped inside.

"It is not to my taste either," Adelia agreed, "though something silver should stand out quite well here."

They moved through the room, opening drawers and pulling back sheets, lifting the rug and ducking to peer into the fireplace. Finally, Duncan felt it safe to say, "I don't think it's in here."

Adelia sighed and bit her lip. "She wouldn't have put it in one of our rooms, of course," she mused.

"Do you think your brother was correct about the library?" Duncan asked.

"Possibly."

"If you continue to gnaw your lip like that, you won't have one left."

His words had the intended effect—she released her lip and smiled. They were very nice lips, Duncan thought, petal pink and full...

He cleared his wandering brain with a brisk shake of his head. "What about the kitchen?" he asked, then answered himself. "But I suppose the staff would find it. That wouldn't do."

"Oh, but they wouldn't!" cried Adelia. "In fact, Mother wouldn't expect anyone to go in the kitchen."

Duncan tried to puzzle this out, but Adelia was already striding toward the door. "It would be the perfect place, really!" she insisted.

He hurried to keep stride with her; she had speed when she wanted it. "No staff in the kitchen?" he asked. "But then where do they cook?"

"Faebourne is enchanted," Adelia explained, "even beyond my mother's curse. Surely you've noticed? We have no established staff, only servants when we need them."

"But then..." Between the swift pace and the strange revelation, he had difficulty pulling his thoughts together. "Where does the food come from?"

"I'm not sure," she admitted. "But all our needs are provided for. Food, clothing... You've seen the wardrobes yourself."

"And the rooms change," mused Duncan.

"Yes, though to what purpose, we've never been sure," said Adelia. "You are the first guest we've had since, well, I don't know how long. At the very least since I was born.

"But it's only the unused rooms that reform themselves," she went on. "We would never have noticed except that we played sardines when we were younger."

"With only three people? Must have been a short game."

"Oh, not when Edward was hiding. We often lost him for hours at a time."

Duncan tried to picture the exuberant Edward staying quiet and still for any length of time. He would have guessed Richard to be the one to blend in. Though, on second thought, it was difficult to imagine Richard Milne playing a children's game to begin with.

They crossed the entry to the back of the house and the stairs that would take them down to the kitchen. Its emptiness felt even stranger to Duncan in the knowledge that there was no staff at all. The long wooden tables, the cold hearth. He wondered whether the larder were barren too. He would find out, he supposed, as they searched.

"But," he said, opening said larder and indeed finding it vacant, "then why did your brother worry about my having a valet?"

"We've never needed servants for guests," said Adelia as she peered into the pots lined up along one of the shelves. Duncan suspected they had never been used. "We've never had any upper servants at all, actually. We dress ourselves, and Faebourne doesn't seem to require the kind of maintenance other large houses demand."

"It cleans itself?"

"Yes."

Duncan moved on to the oversized hearth. No ash in which to hide a knife or any other object for that matter. He peered up the chimney in case there was a niche or some such spot suitable for concealing the weapon. His voice, when he spoke, echoed upward. "So you have footmen to serve the meals, wherever they come from, and a groom for the coach... Someone to tend the horses?"

"As with the servants, we only have horses when we need them. Though I'm sure Faebourne is taking care of your friend's horses," she hastened to add.

Duncan ducked back out of the hearth. "You've never

thought it odd?" he asked. "Food and people and horses out of thin air?"

"Why should I? It's all I've ever known. It's actually quite convenient."

But lonely, Duncan thought, though he was obliged to concede her points. He scanned the bare tables, and the clean, if uneven, stone floor. "Is there anywhere else down here the knife might be?"

Adelia glanced at the equally empty sink and shook her head. "I really thought Mother might have—"

A high-pitched noise brought her words to an abrupt halt. At first Duncan believed a loose hinge was squeaking somewhere; he turned back to the larder to be sure he'd latched it. Then he realized it was a whine. Like that of an injured animal.

Adelia began to scream.

The loudest, most ear-splitting noise to which Duncan had ever been subjected.

He flew to her side, thinking she had been hurt somehow. Also, possibly, to make her stop screeching.

Then he saw and only just managed to bite back a yelp of his own.

Aloysius.

He lay at the foot of the kitchen stairs.

With a silver knife stuck in his shoulder.

CHAPTER 33

"What's this room about?" George asked.

He stood shoulder-to-shoulder with Davies on the threshold of the Green Room. Well, nearly, seeing that he was a little bit taller than his companion. He tried not to notice their proximity, instead focusing on the overwhelmingly green space before them. But he didn't move, either, because part of him—a part he was reluctant to acknowledge—relished the closeness.

"Looks like it was meant to be a gallery. Or ballroom," said Davies. George noticed he didn't move either. Encouragement? Or merely wishful thinking? A misstep would ruin him.

"Pretty useless," he said. "Looks ridiculous with all that furniture clustered there and the rest of it empty."

"Well, then," Davies said, finally stepping into the room, "it shouldn't take us long to examine it." He strolled over to one of the settees and slid his hand into the seam between the back and the seat.

"Don't do that!" said George. "If the knife really is in there, you'll cut yourself."

Davies withdrew the hand. "Wouldn't do to bleed all over the upholstery," he agreed.

"That is not what I'm worried about," George said. He shuffled into the room and approached the opposite settee, halfheartedly lifting one of the bolster pillows that ran along the arm.

"You don't appear keen to find this knife," Davies remarked as he moved on to an armchair.

"My chief concern is what it might be used for," said George.

"We already have the blood."

"What if they need more?" George asked, his agitation spiking. "The whole thing is so—" He threw up his hands.

Davies stopped and stared at him. "Your hackles really are up."

"Aren't yours?" George demanded. "If they go after anyone, it's likely to be you!"

"I'll fret about that if and when it happens. I'm more eager to see it done before we get trapped here somehow." He ducked to see under the small table beside the chair.

"You think she glued it under the table?"

"Not really, but it never hurts to be thorough," Davies said, straightening. He put a hand to his neck to give it a rub.

"Looks like it does," said George. He lifted the second bolster to reveal only more settee. "This is a waste of time."

Without answering, Davies proceeded to the fireplace, leaving the second chair to George. "She wouldn't put it in the furniture," George reasoned. "Unless she hoped someone might accidentally sit on it."

Davies ran his hands over the white marble mantel. They were nice hands, George thought. Deft. Probably quick for doing up buttons. Or *un*doing them.

He heaved a sigh and Davies turned. "Is there a problem?"

Yes. "No. Other than— " He swept a hand to indicate the room, the situation, all of Faebourne and its inhabitants. *I'm sorry I met you because now I'll always know what I can't have.*

To his surprise, Davies gave an answering sigh. "The whole thing is more than a little odd, I grant you. But if we're ever going to get Mr. Oliver home, we have to go along and see it to its end. Whatever that might be."

"So long as it's not the end of you. Or me. Or Duncan."

Davies pursed his lips, and George suspected he did so on purpose to keep from smiling. "In that order?"

George inhaled deeply and tried to determine whether a truthful answer would wreck him. Would Davies be disgusted?

"Yes," he finally said, "I believe so."

Davies' eyes narrowed, and to George's relief he appeared more thoughtful than repulsed. "I could say I wish we'd met under other circumstances," he mused, "but if none of this had happened, we might never have met at all."

George rocked on his feet in an attempt to appear nonchalant rather than nearly knocked down by the valet's words. "When you told Montcliffe I was a friend...?"

"I like to think you are. That is, I hope so. Any friend of Mr. Oliver's and all. Though, the stories he tells about you..." Davies shook his head.

"Don't believe everything Duncan says," warned George.

"Well, now I have my own familiarity to go on."

"You can't count so few hours as the full George Fitzbert experience."

One of Davies' eyebrows inched upward. "No? It's been almost three days."

"But time is different here."

"You're right; I feel like I've known you for years."

"Do you consider that unfortunate?"

There was a moment—it felt dreadfully long to George, though in retrospect it probably lasted mere seconds—before Davies opened his mouth to reply. But before any words came out, the screaming began.

Both he and Davies flinched where they stood, and then Davies did the extraordinary thing of running *towards* the sound.

Every instinct in George urged him to do just the opposite, but he forced his feet to follow Davies. The valet paused in the entry hall then swiveled toward the back of the house as the screaming subsided. George took steps after him but halted as Richard clambered down the stairs calling, "What's happened?"

"I don't know," George told him.

Edward and Odette hurried down after Richard.

Richard passed George in the entry. "Adelia!"

"It was coming from—" George began, but Richard was already striding in the same direction Davies had gone.

Edward and Odette reached the entry but neither showed an inclination to continue onward. Odette stopped at the foot of the stairs and stood wringing her hands, her apprehension writ across her features. Brow furrowed with either concern or puzzlement, Edward walked over to where George was rooted. "What—?"

George broke in, "What's back there?"

Edward's frown deepened. "Downstairs? The kitchen."

"Good a place as any for a knife," muttered George thoughtfully. "Maybe we should—" But before he could suggest venturing farther, the sound of feet on the stairs echoed up into the entry.

Richard emerged first, carrying before him a limp orange object that George did not immediately recognize as Aloysius. Davies followed right behind, his expression grim. Then came a weeping Adelia, Duncan beside her. He kept putting a hand out as though to console her, stopping himself just shy of actually touching her.

Something silver glinted in the russet fur, and George couldn't prevent himself from gasping aloud. Odette's hands disengaged one another and flew to her mouth.

"Is that—?" George began, but he didn't know what to ask. *Aloysius? The knife?*

"He's still alive," said Richard, swerving into the dining room. The group reluctantly trailed him and assembled around the dining table where Richard gently laid the fox.

Aloysius whined softly.

Adelia sobbed loudly.

"Who...?" George murmured.

"We cannot pull it out until we are ready to tend the wound," Richard said. "We will need bandages, needle, thread, hot water... Well?" he demanded when everyone stood staring.

Duncan jolted as Adelia turned, clutched his coat, and buried her face in it. With a cautious glance at Richard, he lightly patted her back.

"Who would do such a thing?" George wondered aloud.

"We must save him," snapped Richard. "Only then will we worry about the rest!"

"The salve," Duncan said suddenly. "It helped my feet. Could it...?"

Adelia drew back and looked up at him then to her eldest brother, her expression lit with hope. Edward wore a similar countenance.

"It is worth trying," Richard decided, but George thought he sounded doubtful.

"If you tell me where it is," said Davies, "along with whatever else is needed, I will fetch them for you."

"I'll help," George added.

"It will all be in a basket on the kitchen table," Adelia said with a sniffle. She looked up at Duncan again. "That is how it works."

George suspected her remark was predicated on some previous conversation, but they hardly had time for it. Davies turned to go, and he did as well. As they exited the dining room, Davies said, "It won't take two of us to carry a basket."

"Yes, well, best to go in pairs in case someone tries to better their aim with another blade."

They walked down the stairs into the subterranean kitchen. The basket sat on one of the long tables, just where Adelia had said it would be. George lingered by the stairs as Davies swiftly cut through the large room.

"Bit strange," George observed.

Davies grabbed the basket. "What's that?"

"No staff."

"Nothing surprises me about this place any more." Supplies in hand, he crossed back to where George stood.

"Who did it, d'you think?" George asked.

"Hard to say." Davies started up the stairs and George went after, not too ashamed to admire the view from behind. "Richard was the only one alone, however."

"Richard?" George yelped, and Davies stopped to look over his shoulder so that George nearly ran right into said view. "But he was so upset just now!"

"Quiet," Davies hissed. "And yes, I know. But perhaps he was upset Aloysius survived."

"But why? He could have hurt Aloysius any time!"

Davies turned and resumed climbing. "I know," he said again with a sigh. "It's not a perfect theory by any stretch."

Their hypothesizing ended as they returned to the dining room. George had not even spared a glance for the basket, but as Davies set it on the table he saw a towel, bandages, the thread and needle, and the small pot that George assumed to be the salve.

"What about the—?" he realized, but before he could finish his question, a glassy-eyed footman entered bearing a steaming kettle. Without a word, he set it on the table and departed.

Richard stroked Aloysius and bent to whisper something to him. He placed his hand on the knife and said to Davies, who still stood next to him, "Be ready with the hot water and a rag." Then he turned to where his sister still clutched Duncan's coat. "Adelia. Thread the needle and be prepared to sew him up."

Adelia swallowed hard, nodded, and retrieved the necessary items from the basket.

"I'm sorry, old friend," Richard said, and for a fleeting moment George wondered whether it was a confession. But then Richard quickly pulled the knife free, and George understood he'd been apologizing for the coming pain.

Aloysius, however, remained remarkably quiet, even as Davies stepped in to wash the wound and Adelia swiftly moved to stitch it.

Duncan extracted the salve from the basket, and when Adelia tied off and snapped the thread, he began to daub the concoction onto the wound. Aloysius' tail twitched. He showed no other sign of discomfort.

Something about the way they worked together, each of them wordlessly tending to his and her task, warmed George. On such short acquaintance, they'd been brought together in a close and friendly—if strange—way. Though with a lurch he noted that he had no part in any of the effort. He'd only stood watching. Useless. He and—

George glanced to his right, where Edward and Odette had hovered, also mere spectators. But they weren't there.

"Erm..." George murmured, unsure of whether their disappearance constituted alarm.

Adelia continued to stroke Aloysius, and Duncan watched the fox as though waiting for something, but Davies and Richard looked over. Richard caught on immediately, his brows snapping together as he demanded, "Where is Edward?"

"They were just here," said George. His gaze met Davies', and he was sure they were both thinking the same thing: *Odette*.

"Where did they go?" Richard asked.

"I don't know. I turned around and they were gone. Maybe they just..." But he could not think of any reason for them to leave or anyplace they might suddenly need to go.

"We have everything now, don't we?" Duncan asked. "For the ritual?"

"Not without Odette," said Davies.

Richard grimaced. "Should have put her in the cauldron."

"Oh, and just how was I supposed to do that?" Duncan asked, his voice low and furious. George observed his friend's fisted hands, the way they shook; he'd never seen Duncan Oliver so angry. "It's all well and good for you to tell me 'do this' and 'do that,' but with little to no instruction—"

"You were *instructed* to use the cauldron," said Richard.

"She has the blood, too," George realized, though he said it so quietly no one seemed to hear.

"And how would *you* stuff a woman into a cauldron?" Duncan went on. "In fact, why not do it yourself?"

"She would not have appeared for me," Richard told him. "If I could save my sister, I would gladly do so, and spare her and the rest of us your bumbling presence!"

A complete and utter hush fell over the dining room. George caught Davies' eye, and they stared at one another, neither daring to move or speak. Then Adelia straightened from where she'd been leaning over Aloysius and said, "Richard. That was inexcusably rude."

Her voice was soft, but it carried in the silence. Richard looked as though she'd slapped him. Without another word, he turned and left the room.

After another moment of silence, George cleared his throat and said again, "She has the blood, too. Odette, that is." He glanced again at Davies, privately hoping no one cited the valet as a potential substitute.

Adelia turned to Duncan. "What should we do?" she asked.

"You're asking *me?*"

"You are my champion."

Duncan turned a despairing look on George and Davies. "I would welcome suggestions."

"Could they be in the house somewhere?" Davies asked.

Duncan countered with, "Why would they leave to begin with?"

Davies grimaced. "To be honest, I don't much trust her myself. Though I cannot express exactly why."

Adelia's eyes widened. "You think she might harm Edward?"

"She might do anything," said George. "And she can look like anyone."

Adelia absently stroked Aloysius, who appeared to have gone to sleep. *He's breathing, at least*, George thought as he watched the fox's side rise and fall. For whatever reason, that simple fact relieved him.

"If they are in the house," said Davies, "they should be easy enough to locate. If not..."

"Back out into the woods," Duncan said with a sigh. He frowned. "That tree..."

When he did not finish the thought, George prompted him. "Tree?"

"Where I found the mirror. And the cauldron. In a cherry tree."

"A cherry tree?" Davies repeated sharply.

Duncan blinked at him. "Yes. That is, I believe it was. I'm no arborist, but..."

Davies turned to George. "Odette spoke of a cherry tree on our ride to Montcliffe. She said she'd 'fallen' from one. I thought it was some kind of joke, but—"

"She may have been dropping tidbits to make herself feel clever," George finished. To Duncan, he said, "I think it's time you guide us on a nature walk."

CHAPTER 34

"It's a good thing we didn't all need grass shoes," remarked George as they walked.

"As things stand, this may be the last outing for those," Davies said, eyeing the frayed footwear that Duncan sported. Duncan's stocking-clad toe was clearly visible through the hole Aloysius had torn in the left slipper.

The sun hung low behind the trees, making the shadows stretch along the path. The day seemed impossibly long to Davies—he supposed it must to George as well, given the difference in time between Faebourne and Birchmere. Their visit to his grandfather felt like it had happened days rather than hours before.

The cauldron swung in time with Duncan's steps. Now and then he transferred it to his other hand. Davies, of a service mindset by habit, considered offering to carry the pot, but something about his employer's demeanor did not invite the proposition. Duncan, Davies understood, was intent on completing the quest on his own terms. Davies and George were mere squires.

"The problem," Duncan said after some time, thus drawing Davies out of the stupor that threatened to overcome him from the monotony of the walk, "is that the path tends to change."

"Change? In what way?" George asked.

"I suppose I shouldn't say 'tends,'" Duncan amended. "This is only my third venture. But it did change between last night and this morning. So it might conceivably change again. In which case, I cannot be sure we'll find the tree."

"Especially if she does not want it to be found," said Davies. He glanced at the trees hanging over them, the spring green leaves bouncing on a slight breeze. "Do you think she has any specific influence over the area?"

Duncan's expression pinched with worry, and he shifted the cauldron again. "I don't know. I have very little comprehension of how any of this works."

They continued on, each bemused by his own thoughts. Davies speculated that, if Odette did have any particular power regarding the path, she would have placed obstacles in their way. But the trail was actually rather pleasant, flat and even, and clear of any stones or roots.

George, it seemed, had been thinking along similar lines. He said, "Or maybe she wants us to find her."

"But why?" Duncan wondered. "Why take Edward? Why..." He waved his free hand. "Why anything?"

"Only she can explain her reasons," said Davies. After a moment, he asked, "You don't think she would harm him, though, do you?"

Neither Duncan nor George answered. Davies marveled at how quickly he'd become accustomed to the strangeness of the situation—a woman who changed shape! Wardrobes that provided clothing! An enchanted house with a staff that literally disappeared when not needed! Two days before, it would have been the stuff of fairy tales, like the stories his mother had read him. But there he was, right in the middle of such a tale.

"She's probably the one who stabbed Aloysius," George said. "The fox knew she was..."

When George didn't supply the word, Davies did. "Evil?"

"Oh, I wouldn't go that far," said Duncan, but then Davies knew his employer well enough to know Duncan Oliver endeavored to see the good in everyone. And if there was none, he could sometimes manufacture it.

The sun sank. The shadows darkened. They walked. Though Davies' eyes were on the path, his mind revisited the old romances his mother had loved—damsels rescued by knights who performed tasks to win both the ladies' freedom and their love. With a start, he wondered whether Duncan *wanted* Adelia's love. He glanced sidelong at his employer as though expecting the answer to be clear on his face. But Duncan only looked vexed and miserable.

"What if we can't do the ritual?" Duncan asked, and all at once Davies understood his distressed countenance. "What if Miss Milne is doomed to become a beast?"

"It won't come to that," George said roundly.

Davies turned, ready to ask how he could possibly know such a thing, but when their gazes met, George shook his head slightly. He didn't know; of course he didn't. He only meant to keep Duncan's spirits up.

Davies pressed his lips together.

Not many steps later, the first petals appeared on the path. They were white, delicate, and scattered, but as the men walked, the carpet of petals thickened until the dirt of the trail could not be seen at all. The dismembered blooms mounded like snowbanks, the perfume of them an instant headache.

Maybe this is her way of stopping us, Davies thought. But if so, it was an ineffectual tactic. They trudged on, slowed but no less determined.

At a bend in the trail, the tree came into view. It was larger—taller, bigger around—than any cherry tree Davies had ever seen. Only a few flowers still clung to the branches. Withering vines curled against the trunk, the blooms on them warped and wrinkled.

Duncan did not stop. Kicking piles of petals before him as though to herald his arrival, he strode directly to the side of the tree and ducked inside. Davies glanced at George, and the two of them followed. But they were still some paces behind when the shrieking began.

"How dare you!" Odette's shrill voice burst from the tree. "How dare you bring that into my home!"

Davies did not catch Duncan's response, but he heard Odette's, "Impossible!" as he achieved the rough-hewn doorway cut into the tree trunk. He paused on the threshold.

Odette stood with her back against the far wall, as far from Duncan as feasible in the small space. It took Davies a moment to recognize her, despite her being the only woman. For the first time since he met her, she did not look like someone assembled from different pieces of various portraits. Rather, she appeared at home and entirely herself. She stood at average height, with auburn hair and calamine eyes that matched the dress she wore. Edward sat on a large cushion, seemingly unhurt. His expression was one of shock and confusion, but on Davies' admittedly brief acquaintance that was not unusual.

Duncan stood just inside the door, his hat too tall to fit under the hanging lantern that lit the room. He had not removed it, an atypical oversight as Davies knew his employer to be keen on good manners. But perhaps with all the other demands on his attention, such things fell to the wayside.

"I would never bring an iron cauldron here!" Odette raged, evidently answering something Duncan had said, and Davies realized her reason for distancing herself from his employer.

"She could not have," Edward supplied. "She was at Faebourne and would not have been able to return to the house if she left it."

Duncan turned to him. "Are you well, Mr. Milne? Your brother and sister are quite concerned for your safety."

Edward's mouth fell open. "I— That is..." Tears became evident in his eyes, though they failed to spill. "Is Aloysius...?"

"He will recover," said Duncan. Then, with a glance at Odette, he added, "To Miss Odette's sorrow, I'm sure."

Odette produced a noise Davies could not name, except to call it an exasperation commingled with denial. "The little beast attacked me!"

"He only took your shoe!" said George from over Davies' shoulder, startling him; he had not realized George was behind him. However, once he knew, he could not unknow it, and his entire back began to feel warm from the awareness of proximity.

"No," Edward said quietly. All heads swiveled his way. "After that. In the library. We found the knife—*I* found it—behind a false back in the desk. Next thing, Aloysius came in, growling and snapping, and I... I... I did try not to hurt him too badly. Only to stop him."

Silence hung over the room for a moment. Then George said —too loudly in Davies' right ear—"*You* stabbed Aloysius?"

Edward dropped his face into his hands.

"That's why you left?" Duncan asked.

"I took him," said Odette.

Edward looked up sharply, seemingly as surprised by this declaration as all the other men in the room.

Odette lifted her chin. "As is my due."

"Your due?" asked Davies.

"Put that thing outside," Odette said with a nod at the cauldron still hanging from Duncan's hand. "Before it kills my tree. Then I will explain our contract with the Milnes of Faebourne."

CHAPTER 35

*D*avies and George stepped back as Duncan moved to set the cauldron just outside the entrance to the cherry tree. Then he removed his hat and went back inside. Odette waved him and his companions toward more of the hassocks, and they each sat, hats in their hands, like children awaiting a story.

Odette settled herself on the stump Duncan had assumed to be a table. It allowed her to sit higher than her guests. "Five generations ago, a man named Ambrose Milne married one of our kind."

"Your kind?" Edward asked.

She cut her eyes in his direction. "No one has told you this story? For shame. A man should always know where he comes from."

Beside Duncan, Davies flinched.

"Fey women do sometimes take mortal husbands," Odette continued. "But they always live in our realm. For a fey woman to agree to live in the mortal world..." She shook her head. "She must have loved him very much.

"As a wedding gift, we gave them Faebourne, which as you must know is built on fey land. The house itself is, as you've seen, enchanted."

The music of Odette's voice entranced Duncan. Without

realizing, he'd begun to lean forward like a tree reaching for sun. "You're fey," he said wonderingly.

"Of course," Odette told him. "Most songs are."

"And is Miss Milne? Her mother thought..."

The corners of Odette's mouth turned down in a moue of distaste. "She is not," she said. "At least, not fully, though of course it runs in the bloodlines. But her mother's madness—the cause of her misconception that her daughter was a changeling— was induced by breaking the contract."

"What contract?" asked Edward.

"In order to marry his fey bride, and for future generations of Milnes to continue living in Faebourne, Ambrose Milne promised that each of those generations would provide the fey with a human child."

"What in blazes would you want with a human baby?" George burst.

Odette frowned at him. "We quite like them. Most of them are affectionate by nature and easy to train."

"Are you saying," said Edward, "that my..." His face wrinkled with thought. "Distant aunts and uncles? That some of them were raised by fairies?"

"Three, to be precise," said Odette. "Including your paternal uncle. It should have been four, but Nathaniel and Tabitha Milne did not honor the agreement."

"Was it meant to be the oldest child?" Davies asked.

Odette shrugged. "It did not have to be. The pact was not specific on that point, and we've noticed humans like to keep their oldest children as a sort of prize."

Duncan turned to Edward. "Your parents had three children, but did not offer any to..." He turned back to Odette.

"The terms of the agreement state the child is to be left here by the cherry tree," she said. "Any time within the first year of its life. Usually, the parents choose to do it early, before they become attached.

"It seemed Nathaniel and Tabitha did not believe the story when Nathaniel's mother told it to them. They thought she'd gone mad."

"You took Edward," Duncan said, "as belated payment towards this contract?"

"But I came willingly!" Edward cried. "You did not have to—" He looked at Duncan, as though to do so helped him remember the word he sought. "Abduct me."

Duncan put his hands to his head in an attempt to hold his thoughts in. "So Tabitha Milne did not give away one of her children. And then?"

Odette cocked her head. "And then Faebourne did what it is meant to do. It whispered to her, tried to convince her to fulfill the obligation. Unfortunately, it appears she misunderstood. Not all humans are receptive to such things."

"Whispering houses, you mean," said George wryly.

Odette's lips twisted with amusement. "Instead of relinquishing her baby, Tabitha Milne became convinced her youngest child was a changeling. And evidently cursed her."

A shroud of silence fell over them. Then Duncan asked, "Where does this leave us? Can the curse be lifted? Will you help us?"

She looked at Edward. "Even if you agree to stay and honor the contract—"

"I will!"

She held up a hand. "It will not change the circumstances of your sister's curse. The ritual is the only way."

"The cauldron," Duncan remembered, "and the mirror. They were both here. This is where I found them."

Odette shook her head. "It is true I had the mirror, though it was whole when I left. As for the cauldron, I do not understand how it could have been here. It would poison my tree. You see how the flowers have fallen."

"Iron is anathema to the fey," said Davies.

George lifted an eyebrow at him. "How do you know that?"

"My mother."

George snorted. "All those stories, eh?"

"That must be why Richard was so insistent on it," Edward said. "He understood what—who, rather," he threw Odette a bashful look, "we were dealing with."

The gentlemen regarded one another.

"Could he have?" Davies asked. "Left the cauldron here?"

"But why?" Edward countered.

"He wanted me to find the cauldron," said Duncan. "He was so insistent. If he came all this way to put it in a tree, why not just bring it back to Faebourne himself?"

"And why break the mirror?" asked George.

They all looked to Odette, who smiled apologetically. "The only person who can answer these questions is Mr. Milne himself."

CHAPTER 36

"**B**ut you will come back with us?" Edward entreated.

"If you honor the contract, I will help you," Odette told him.

"Rather mercenary of you," remarked George as he rose awkwardly from the pouf on which he'd been ensconced. "To ask for people to give up their children so you can raise them as pets or some such..." He shook his head and tapped his hat back onto it before turning for the exit. The space felt too close, too warm. Part of that was due to the bodies—so many in such a small space. A larger part might have emanated from the acute awareness of Davies sitting beside him. But the largest portion of heat sprang from his anger.

It surprised him, yet Odette's explanation had affected him badly. That fairies existed? Well, all right. With everything he'd witnessed, he could believe that. But that they demanded such tribute just because someone had the ill luck to fall in love outside the bounds of humanity?

Falling in love outside accepted norms was the story of his life.

He was down the path, around the bend, and out of view in a trice. He barely noticed the petals, now gleaming softly in the growing twilight. *Romantic*, he thought, but the word felt spiteful in his mind. He kicked at some of the petals to see if that would cheer him. It didn't.

"Fitzbert!" And then more breathlessly, "George!"

The sound of his Christian name struck him like a thrown pebble, the more because of who spoke it. He turned to see Davies hurrying to catch him up.

"You can't go wandering out here alone," Davies admonished.

"It's a clearly marked trail," said George. "Anyway, if Duncan can manage it, so can I." He kick some more petals, but his anger continued to simmer.

He could feel Davies' gaze, intent and perceptive. To escape it, he turned and began to walk again. But Davies fell into step beside him.

"We don't understand their ways," Davies said. "Their... culture."

"Stealing children is a culture now?"

"We don't have any reason to believe the children are harmed."

"But the parents must be!" George insisted. "To have to give over a child, not know his or her fate, never see it again!" He stopped and looked at Davies, though the blackening shadows made it difficult to see more than the glint of the valet's dark eyes and the white of his shirt. "If it had been me and Henry, how could my parents have chosen between us?"

"And yet some parents exile their children quite deliberately," Davies retorted, "without fairies or anyone else to care for them."

"You are angry on your mother's behalf," said George. "Even though the connection has been reestablished."

"And you are angry on behalf of a hypothetical that does not touch you at all," said Davies. "Or is it that you wish to avenge the Milnes?"

"Every generation of that family has been forced to honor a contract they never agreed to!"

"Well, Edward Milne appears perfectly willing to—"

"And if Duncan and Miss Milne marry and have children?"

Davies rocked and took a step back, apparently momentarily stunned. After taking a moment to catch his wits, he said,

"Then that is something they must decide between themselves."

"Will they ever see Edward again?"

"I don't know!" Davies burst. "It's not my place to know, nor is it yours. One cannot spend one's life worrying about things that may or may not happen, or—or—other people's lives!"

"That's it, then, is it?" George asked. "You plan to go sit at Montcliffe and never think about anyone else?"

"I haven't decided what I will do," Davies told him, "but once again, you are concerned about things which do not impact you. Do you not have enough in your own life to keep you occupied?"

"*You* are in my life!"

The air of the forest suddenly seemed very quiet around them. George was grateful it had become too dark to clearly see his companion's face.

"And Duncan," George added, seeking to cover his indiscretion. "If you go off to Montcliffe and he falls sway to Faebourne..."

"We do not know his intentions," said Davies. His voice sounded strained, though George supposed he could be imagining it. "But even if he did marry Miss Milne, he would surely take her to Dove Hill."

"Where I never go."

"Still on about that, are you?" The thread of amusement in his tone relieved George. "Well, the offer to visit Montcliffe stands. Assuming I do inherit."

"You would accept the title?"

"A man should know where he comes from," said Davies, echoing Odette's earlier words.

"That doesn't exactly ans—"

"There you are!" Duncan's voice sounded unnaturally loud on the night air. "We thought you were lost."

"We're on the path," Davies pointed out as Duncan, Edward, and Odette approached. Duncan had brought the cauldron, George noted, though he held it on the opposite side of where Odette walked.

Despite the gloom, Duncan seemed to notice George's attention. "It is needed for the ritual."

Irrational and blazing, George's anger flooded back. "Just what is this ritual? Where is it from? Where is the curse from, for that matter?" He thrust a forefinger at Odette. "You expect us to believe Tabitha Milne had some mystic ability to turn her daughter into a beast? You've already said she could not understand Faebourne when it spoke to her!"

But it was Edward who answered. "Books," he said sadly. "Our library was full of strange, old books. Heirlooms. Mummy became obsessed with them. The spell came from one of those. Eventually Richard packed them all away somewhere because he felt they were making her—her affliction worse. "

George fancied Odette looked triumphant. She said to him, "I understand you do not approve of my kind or our way of doing things. But take a moment to consider that you yourself know what it is like to be condemned, if not directly then implicitly, and for something over which you exercise no control."

Duncan frowned at her. "I don't follow."

"No," she agreed, "but he does."

Duncan turned with what George took to be a questioning look, though in the near dark it was difficult to tell. He ignored it, just as he pretended not to see Davies' thoughtful frown. Instead, he simply turned again in the direction of Faebourne. "Sooner there, sooner done with all this," he said and started off at a long stride, leaving the others to follow.

CHAPTER 37

*T*hough he realized he shouldn't let George go off alone again, Davies felt rooted to the place where he stood. All he could do was watch George's retreating form as the shadows swallowed it.

Odette's voice nearby broke the temporary paralysis. "I think," she said, "you may also understand my meaning."

He turned to find her at his shoulder. Despite the fall of night, which left everyone else's faces partially obscured, she appeared to glow. Only faintly, but enough to make her expression clear. That same knowing, provoking look he'd seen on her before.

"Am I to assume you would choose differently if you could?" he asked her. "That you would not hold the Milnes to this agreement if you had a choice?"

She tilted her head to regard him. "Would you be different if you could choose?"

"There is a difference between enforcing a cruel covenant and choosing to be, say, fey at all to begin with."

She held his gaze a moment longer before nodding. "The difference between being who you are and being forced into painful arrangements," she said. Davies fancied he heard a snatch of pianoforte music underscoring her words.

"He's a very good valet," Duncan said suddenly. He turned to

Davies. "Though of course I understand your choosing another course now that one has been presented to you. I do hope serving me wasn't *so* painful an arrangement. You will make a fine addition to the peerage."

Davies blinked, unable to formulate a response that would put his employer—nay, friend—at ease without compromising the true meaning of his conversation with Odette. "We should not let Fitzbert get too far ahead," was all he said.

Luckily, George had not kept up the speedy pace with which he'd departed. If anything, he appeared to be tiring by the time Davies caught up, the others not far behind. George glanced at him as he fell into step alongside but did not say anything. The remainder of the walk back to Faebourne occurred in silence save for the shuffle of feet and the sighing of the evening air through the tree branches. A half moon unmasked itself from behind the silhouetted leaves and lent light to the apron of lawn as the house finally came into view. Without a word, Duncan removed the grass slippers and handed them to Odette for her use. Then, by yet another word-less accord, they prompted Edward to the front of their assembly and he led them inside.

"Adelia?" Edward called as they entered through the back veranda and walked to the front entry hall. His thin and some-what reedy voice bounced back at them. "Richard?"

Adelia appeared in the doorway to the Small Room, Aloysius cradled in her arms. His eyes were open, and he seemed to Davies to be much improved, though he supposed that was little enough. Having been stabbed counted rather as a nadir in one's day, if not life. Assuming one survived, improvement was not difficult.

Adelia, however, looked the worse—her pale skin yellow and wan, her silvery hair beginning to fall from its pins in lank strings rather than shining waves. Her feverish blue eyes fastened on her brother, but she said nothing.

Edward understood all the same. "He told you."

"How could you?" Adelia rasped. Her gaze shifted to Odette. "And you. Why have you come back? Why—" she rounded on Duncan, "have you brought her back?"

When Duncan failed to respond except to let his mouth fall open, Davies spoke. "She is needed for the ritual."

For a moment Adelia only stared at him. Her entire body shook with fury, her pale cheekbones blazed with heat. At last, she commanded, "Then put her in the cauldron! Do not allow this creature to walk free in our home!"

Edward stepped forward, hands up in supplication. "Adelia, please. She's agreed to help us. To help *you*."

"For a price," George murmured.

Adelia whirled on him next. "At what cost?"

George's amber eyes shifted in Edward's direction.

Edward cleared his throat. But instead of explaining, he asked, "Where is Richard?"

"I have not seen him," said Adelia.

"Did he leave the house last night?" Duncan asked.

She looked at him as if his wits had flown, but before she could answer, Richard's voice sounded from across the entry: "I did."

The party turned to see him framed by the open double doors of the Green Room. His arms were crossed, his expression as dour as ever. "I went to fetch the cauldron," he said, "but the house would not allow me to bring it back."

"So you put it in the tree," Duncan said.

Richard did not deny it.

"Why?" Edward asked.

Richard's eyes slid to where Odette stood. "You tried to kill my tree," she said.

"I tried to save my family," Richard told her. "When I found the tree, I knew the old story was true. I thought there might be a way to break the covenant."

"If the tree no longer existed..." said Duncan.

"Nowhere to leave the babies," George finished. "You knew about the agreement?" he asked Richard.

"When Mother told me, I thought it was part of her madness," said Richard. "I saw no reason to repeat it to my siblings. Even if it was true—as it seems it was—it was too late to do anything about it."

"But the mirror?" Davies asked. "Why break it? Didn't you

know it was needed for the ritual? You knew your sister's afflic-tion was real enough."

Richard's gaze settled on him, somehow cold and hot at once. "The house would not allow me to bring it back, either. I tried to bring back smaller pieces instead, but—" He pursed his lips, seemingly unwilling to admit his full failure.

Ah, thought Davies, *he discarded the shards on the path when he could not bring them home.*

"Will it work if it's broken?" Edward asked.

"Your brother's instincts were correct," answered Odette. "A mirror functions regardless of the number of pieces it is in; one only requires a shard. In this case, the mirror in question is designed to show one's true self." She smiled at Richard in the same knowing way she'd done at Davies before, and he noted she had begun to change again. Her hair had turned red-gold in a shade similar to Edward's, her eyes a soft brown, her dress jonquil. It seemed that somehow, when she left her home, she could not retain her true shape—she was forced to adopt a guise. Would the fairy mirror show her differently? "This is why it is needed for the ritual," she went on. She turned to Adelia with an almost apologetic smile. "The mirror will show whether the beast your mother created in you remains. In short, it will show whether the ritual is successful."

Duncan's brow furrowed and his mouth thinned. Davies recognized the expression as the one his (soon to be former) employer often wore when faced with an unpleasant task. Duncan Oliver avoided confrontation whenever possible, but he also had a determined streak; he kept his promises and did what he thought right. Davies admired these qualities. He could not have so willingly served anyone less honorable.

"We must gather the items," Duncan declared.

"The mirror is still here," said Adelia, indicating the Small Room behind her. She grimaced and drew Aloysius closer to her. "I left the knife in the dining room."

George strode toward the dining room doors. "I'll fetch it."

"I have the cauldron," Duncan added, holding up the pot still in his hand. He looked to Odette. "You have the blood?"

She nodded and, to Davies' amazement, withdrew a small

glass vial from the inner cuff of her sleeve. Either the glass itself was dark in color, or the contents were—perhaps both. Davies could not distinguish.

"And you *are* the song," he said. He looked first at Richard, who had not moved, then to Adelia. "That is everything?"

"Except the book," said Edward. "Which details the ritual."

They all turned to Richard then, even as George re-emerged from the dining room with the silver knife gleaming in his fist. Richard only stared back until Adelia asked, "Richard?"

"I do not have it," he told her.

"You stored it somewhere?" Edward asked. "Well, I suppose we'll have to—"

"I burned them," said Richard. "All of them."

CHAPTER 38

For a moment it felt as if the room had been robbed of air. George felt positively lightheaded as they stood in the entry, staring at Richard. Finally, Edward asked the question none of them seemed able to catch enough breath to utter: "Why?"

Richard's countenance grew grimmer—something George had not thought possible. Yet the eldest Milne did not speak.

"When?" Adelia asked, her voice thin and wavering.

Without waiting for Richard to answer, Duncan said, "You mean to say you let us go through all this——" He waved the hand not holding the cauldron. "To no benefit?"

Richard's face fell then, collapsing into sorrow as he looked to his sister. "I am sorry, Adelia. I did not believe he would succeed."

"When?" she asked again, stronger than before.

"Years ago," Richard admitted. "Mother was so fixated. I would sneak them out a few at a time and burn them in the kitchen fireplace."

"But the list of items..." Edward said.

Adelia turned her wide, blue eyes on him, her expression evincing horror at whatever thought had just struck her. "Have you ever seen it?" When Edward only blinked at her, she added, "The list!"

"Well, no, but…"

Again all heads swiveled toward Richard.

"The list is true," he insisted. "That much I memorized. Adelia," he said again, "we were young, and I truly thought Mother had…" He drew in a deep breath. "I did not think the curse was real. The effects, as you recall, only became evident later. I wanted to—to—" He flexed his fists at his sides as he sought the words. George supposed Richard Milne was not particularly articulate by nature, not given much to conversation in the normal course of things. Whatever counted as normal at Faebourne.

Richard forged on. "I wanted to be rid of everything that provoked her malady. I thought by getting rid of the books, they would lose their hold over her and she…" His face twisted with grief. "She would get better."

"And now your sister cannot get better," Duncan growled, "because we haven't the text we need to aid her."

Easy enough for Duncan to be angry, George thought. Seeing that Richard had more than once shown a lack of faith in Duncan's abilities, George could somewhat empathize with his friend's ire. But Richard looked so miserable that George couldn't help but feel sorry for him. "At least he remembered the list," he offered in weak support.

"Assuming his memory is any better than his judgement," snapped Duncan.

George recoiled. He had never seen his mild-mannered friend so agitated. He glanced at Davies who likewise frowned in Duncan's direction.

"Tongue lashing a man over his youthful follies does nothing to solve our present crisis," Davies said, and George inwardly cheered the would-be lord's level head. "To the best of our knowledge, we have the necessary items. We know that the mirror will show us the outcome once the ritual is performed. We can reasonably guess that the blood and music are to be combined in the cauldron in some way?" He looked around for affirmation.

"And the knife?" Edward asked.

George, having forgotten he held it, was so startled he nearly dropped it.

No one answered.

"Well, if we don't know..." Duncan began testily.

Odette cleared her throat in the light, polite way George thought of as peculiar to women hoping to draw attention. Once everyone had turned her way, she said, "I may know."

"You know the ritual?" Edward asked, his colorful eyes lighting with hope.

"Not specifically," she answered, "but I know enough about fairy spells in general to guess."

"And if you guess wrong?" Duncan asked. "You cannot trifle with Miss Milne's well-being!"

"I think that is a decision Miss Milne must make for herself," said Davies. "Whether to risk it, that is."

Adelia smiled at him, and something in George faltered and began to doubt. But no, he'd read enough fairy stories—not, perhaps, as many as Davies, or even Henry, but enough—to know how they ended. Adelia Milne and her champion would live happily ever after. Assuming, of course, she did not turn into a heraldic beast.

A glance at Duncan's frowning countenance, however, told George that his doubts about Adelia and Duncan's assured happy ending were shared. And doubts shared were doubts doubled. George looked at Richard—if anyone might gauge Adelia's affections, surely it would be he—but he only continued to look wretched.

"I trust you," Adelia said, still beaming at the valet, and a pang like an arrow shot through George's chest. She trusted Davies, not Duncan. Not even her brothers. Well, and why should she trust them if one stabbed her fox and the other burned the books that would save her? George sighed. Davies was the most capable and trustworthy of all of them. Of course Adelia Milne wanted him.

But what—or who—did Davies want?

As ever, he was infuriatingly impossible to read. His face a polite blank. Damn his mannered upbringing. George had the sudden urge to go shake a reaction out of him. He only clinched the knife more tightly and forced his feet to remain rooted. He would not be a poor loser, even though there was nothing and no one he'd ever wanted more in life.

But then Adelia turned her smile on all of them, like a ray of light sweeping the room. "All of you," she said. "We have to at least try. Oh!" In her arms, Aloysius began to squirm, and she was forced to set him down lest she drop him. The fox appeared to have mended, a winding bandage looped around him the only sign he had ever been injured; he moved smoothly and without any sign of pain. He walked to the door of the Small Room and looked back at them expectantly.

"There," said Adelia, "Aloysius trusts you, too. And there is no one whose judgement I depend upon more."

"Well, then," said Duncan, but his lips were still thin with suppressed umbrage, "no use putting it off. If you are ready, Miss Milne, let us attempt to break this spell."

George thought her smile, when aimed at Duncan, was a mite sad. "Whatever happens, please know that I am grateful to you as my champion." And with that she swept off after Aloysius into the Small Room.

After a moment during which none of them were quite able to meet another's eyes, the rest of them followed.

CHAPTER 39

*D*uncan could not remember ever being so furious, though he suspected his anger was misplaced. He understood, rationally, that the circumstances were the root of his ire. Richard was not really to blame; he'd not acted out of malice when he burned the books all those years ago—quite the opposite, in fact. Davies had been correct, too, in pointing out the fruitlessness of his outrage. But knowing this—along with the memory of Adelia's smile bestowed like a gift on his valet—only irritated Duncan all the more.

So he set the cauldron none too gently on the table in the Small Room, causing the remains of the mirror to rattle. It appeared Adelia had attempted to reassemble the collected shards like a puzzle, though there were a number of gaps. At least Odette had confirmed the glass did not need to be intact to work.

The gathering ranged themselves to stand in a circle around the table: Aloysius at the feet of his mistress, Duncan beside her, then Davies, Odette, Edward, George, and finally Richard, who trailed in as though unsure of his welcome then came to stand between Adelia and George.

Odette then handed the vial she held to Davies. When he looked questioningly at her, she said, "I will have to go in..." She seemed unable to finish the sentence and so pointed at the cauldron.

"You must pour the blood in after me," Odette went on. She turned to George. "Pour it over the knife blade as it goes into the..." This time she indicated the pot with a jerk of her chin.

"Then what?" asked George.

"Then it works. Or it doesn't."

"Are there magic words or something?" Edward asked.

Odette smiled at him the fond way a mother might a child who has asked an amusing question. "*I* am the magic words."

Edward's mouth fell into a little "o." Then he asked, "But will you come back?"

This time her smile stretched with genuine pleasure. "I must if I'm to take you with me."

"Take him?" Adelia asked.

"That is the, uh, price," said Edward.

"For what?" Richard demanded, and Duncan was amazed by the immediate change in him. From quiet and withdrawn to forbidding in an instant.

"Oh, Edward, if this is to help me—" Adelia began.

"It is for Faebourne," Edward said. "I don't mind. I—" He looked at Odette. "I think I might enjoy it."

"But will we see you?" Adelia asked.

For the first time, Odette appeared uncomfortable. "It is not usually permitted."

"Not usually," echoed Davies. "Which means it sometimes is."

Odette rewarded him with vexed look. "Yes," she admitted.

"If he does not agree to this, we will lose Faebourne?" Richard asked.

"Faebourne is fey," Odette told him, "it seeks to honor the pact made between us and your family. It will begin to behave increasingly erratically and possibly drive you all as mad as your mother."

The Milne siblings winced at her candidness.

"But if we left," Richard said.

"If this works," Duncan put in, "and Miss Milne is *able* to leave, that is."

Richard nodded, conceding Duncan's point. "Best get on with it then."

Odette closed her eyes and began to hum. But George hastily asked, "How will we know if it's worked?"

She opened one eye to see him. "Check the mirror." Then she closed the eye and gave herself over to her song.

As Odette hummed, Duncan felt warm all over, as though wrapped in a blanket. The sensation made him drowsy, and his eyelids began to fall. He swayed where he stood and did not realize his vision had gone grey until a gasp from Edward returned him to awareness. His sight cleared just in time to see Odette dissolve into the nothingness.

The sound of her humming remained, however. At first it seemed to hang in the air, but then it moved into the cauldron, the song becoming hollow as it bounced off the curved innards of the iron pot.

George and Davies exchanged a glance and by unspoken agreement each stepped forward. George held the knife out over the cauldron and Davies unstoppered the vial. He poured the thick, reddish-brown liquid over the blade and into the pot.

The music stopped.

They waited, George poised with the dripping blade.

Nothing.

With trembling hands, Adelia bent to pick up the mirror. She held it flat to prevent the shards from spilling and leaned over to look. Standing beside her, Duncan spied the reflection: golden fur over a sharp muzzle and a fleeting glimpse of feathers before Adelia stifled a sob and dropped the mirror back onto the table, the neatly arranged slivers jostling out of place.

"I take that to mean it didn't work," said George. Duncan glared at him.

"Maybe there wasn't enough blood," suggested Edward.

"Or it's the wrong kind," Richard said. "A blade like that doesn't want external blood. It wants something fresh." His gaze settled on Davies, and George whisked the knife aside, not heeding the droplets of blood that fell to the rug.

"If that were true," said George, "Miss Odette would have told us."

"Would she?" Duncan asked. "Perhaps she didn't know." He looked at his valet. Damned if Davies weren't the knight of the story after all, the true champion. "I'd do it myself if I could," Duncan told him. "But I'm afraid in this case we must ask for your help."

Davies' lips twitched, and to Duncan's surprise he appeared amused. "As your squire?"

"As Miss Milne's hero," said Duncan.

Davies' face grew serious. "That I cannot be, I'm afraid." He gave a small bow in Adelia's direction. "Forgive me, Miss Milne. I am happy—honored, even—to help you. But I am not the one to save you."

"Davies!" Duncan exclaimed. "You just said—"

But the valet ignored him, instead turning to George. "Give me the knife."

Duncan frowned, confused. "Are you going to do it or aren't you?"

Meanwhile, George stepped sideways, putting Edward between them once more. "Why?"

"Because," said Davies, "while Mr. Milne's memory is no doubt very good, it is not infallible. Come, Fitzbert. We do not know if Miss Odette can remain in the cauldron indefinitely."

With clear reluctance, George handed the knife over. Duncan had never seen his normally carefree friend so tense, so worried. "I hope you're certain of what you're doing," George said.

Davies did not answer him. In one swift movement, he reached over and grabbed Duncan's wrist. Before Duncan could demand what he was doing, Davies had his hand over the cauldron. With a quick, sure stroke, he cut Duncan's palm open.

"That stings!" said Duncan.

"I'd be surprised if it didn't," said Davies, his tone far too mild for Duncan's liking. Duncan started to protest, but Davies hushed him.

The blood welled from the slash and trickled into the cauldron.

Davies released him, though Duncan kept his hand suspended over the pot to keep from bleeding elsewhere.

They waited.

After a moment, Duncan felt it. At first he thought it was because of the cut, that perhaps he was becoming lightheaded. But then a heat began to crawl over his body—not the cozy warmth he'd experienced previously, but a prickling like many tiny embers burning the entirety of his skin. At the same time he heard a high-pitched aria. It did not emanate from the cauldron, but came from seemingly everywhere. Indeed, Duncan looked around, trying to pinpoint the sound that was beautiful and painful at once. A scan of the faces around him, however, showed none of them heard or felt what he did. They all only frowned quizzically at him, watching, still waiting.

A mist began to swirl in the cauldron. The aria swelled and fell into the pot where it faded. The mist drifted out and slowly took the shape of Odette—her true self, as they'd seen her in the cherry tree. She smiled and said to Adelia, "Look."

Blinking like one just awakened, Adelia reached again for the mirror. This time her reflection brought tears to her eyes.

Unable to see it this time from where he stood, Duncan asked, "Miss Milne?"

She dropped the mirror again, ignoring its jangle. Then she threw her arms around his neck. "Thank you, Mr. Oliver!" Arms still firmly in place, she turned and added, "And to you, Mr. Davies."

"Oh dear," said Edward. "The rug." Adelia's enthusiasm had forced Duncan to move his hand which, though not bleeding as freely as before, still trailed droplets of blood. Duncan strove to hold the hand away from everyone as well as the furniture lest he mar any fabrics. The rug, however, could not be helped.

"How?" George asked. He looked at Davies as though seeing him for the first time. "How did you know?"

"The blood of a lord," said Davies. "It made no sense to me." He shrugged. "Mr. Oliver was clearly meant to be Miss Milne's champion, so I could not be the solution to her dilemma. However, if one considered the blood of a lord to be *noble*..." He looked at Richard. "I thought, perhaps, you may have remembered the list incorrectly after all. It might have said 'noble' blood rather than specifying the blood of a lord."

"I still don't understand," Duncan said. "I'm not noble."

"You're not a lord," said Davies, "but you're noble of heart. You're her champion."

Something bloomed in Duncan's chest like a flower. He felt as though he'd just been given a priceless gift. "Thank you," he said. The words seemed inadequate, but he did not know what else to say.

Davies appeared to understand. He smiled and dropped the knife into the cauldron. "We should probably bandage that," he said with a nod at Duncan's hand.

"The salve is still in the dining room," said Adelia. She released Duncan's neck and took his uninjured hand.

More flowers opened inside him, more heat pricked his skin. He suspected he was blushing. But he allowed her to lead him out of the room. He felt high as a kite, and she was the string that anchored him. Or perhaps the wind that caused him to rise?

Still not a poet, he thought.

But he was something better.

He was a hero.

CHAPTER 40

*T*he dining room table held not only the salve and basket of supplies but a spread of platters piled with cheeses, fruit, cold meats, and freshly baked bread. Davies had not realized how hungry he was until he saw and smelled the food. So while Adelia sat tending Duncan's hand, the rest of the party stood and grazed.

"When will you go?" George asked Edward.

Edward in turn looked to Odette. "I'm already late as it is, given I was supposed to be handed over at birth."

"Would it have been you?" Davies asked. "That is, if parents usually keep the first child, do they then always give up the second?" This true-life fairy world intrigued him; he wondered how different it was from the stories. Were any of the tales accurate?

"Not necessarily," Odette said. "Sometimes they have several sons and then give away a daughter. I've noticed they more readily give away the girls." She looked across the table at where Adelia wrapped bandages across Duncan's palm.

"What if there is only one child?" George asked. "Must they still give it up?"

"How could they know there won't be more?" Davies countered. "If the child is meant to be given up within the first year, and the parents are thinking they will wait and give up the next child..."

George looked to Odette. "Is that when you steal them?"

"We've also been known to return them," she said. "Though they have difficulty adapting to the human world after living so long in ours." Her gaze drifted again to Adelia. "I do worry for her."

"For Miss Milne?" Davies asked, his gaze following hers. Adelia and Duncan were smiling, talking, oblivious to anything around them, including Aloysius, who stood on the next chair to steal grapes from the table. "Why?"

"She only knows Faebourne. It's as good as having been raised in the fairy lands."

"If so, why must you take Edward?" Richard asked. His low voice, heretofore unheard, made Davies jump with surprise. "We have all of us been raised here, and as you've said, this land, this house, is fey."

"But you were not willingly given," Odette said.

"Edward is willing," said George, slowly and thoughtfully, and Davies eyed him, watching his mind work. "But... can't he just live here?"

Odette paused. "Well, that's never been... That is, I don't... I don't know."

"It's not a matter of raising him," Davies pointed out. "So what would the fey do with him if he lived there? Would it be anything that could not be accomplished here?"

"Well, he must be presented at the fairy court," said Odette, "to Queen Laudine."

"He can live here for that, can't he?" Davies asked.

"They will expect him to be active in our world," Odette went on. "Part of our society. We often..." She blushed and ducked her head. "We often marry our humans." Then, lifting her head again in defiance, she added, "It is good to have fresh bloodlines, you see. Our world is rather small. It's one of the reasons we make these kinds of bargains and sometimes exchange children."

From where he stood in a corner nibbling a piece of cheese, Edward said quietly, "I don't mind. Really, I don't mind going."

"I mind!" roared Richard, causing Adelia and Duncan to turn abruptly from their conversation. "I have no desire to remain at Faebourne alone."

"Why, Richard, you can go anywhere you like," Adelia told him. "Back to London, or—"

"I did not care for London."

"You were hardly there," said Duncan. "I am sure there are parts of it you might enjoy. But perhaps you would like to come to Dove Hill?"

"Oh no you don't!" said George. "You don't go inviting someone you just met to Dove Hill when you've never asked me!"

Duncan looked at him blankly. "Haven't I? Well, I suppose I just assumed you knew you were always welcome." He turned his smile back to Adelia. "Miss Milne has agreed to visit, and she will require a chaperone."

"Me?" George scoffed.

"I believe he meant Miss Milne's brother," Davies said.

"Very well," said Richard, making it sound as if he were acceding to a burdensome favor. "After all, Adelia cannot go out into society unattended."

"And perhaps you will find someone to keep you company at Faebourne," Edward told his brother. His expression became uncertain as he looked to Odette. "Will we be able to visit?"

She took a deep breath. "I believe so. This is an unusual circumstance, and I am sure we can plead your case to the Queen. She is not insensitive to these things.

"We will stay the night here, I think," Odette went on. "You need not bring anything—we will provide your essentials—but if you would like to take a few personal items, you may."

Things were squaring off nicely, Davies thought, though he supposed he needed to formally give his notice. He opened his mouth to do just that, but Duncan forestalled him. "I know," he said. "But I do hope you will visit. It's going to be devilish difficult to replace you."

"We'll leave in the morning?" George asked, and when Davies' eyebrows lifted, he said, "*I'm* the one with a curricle and horses, as I recall. Unless you plan to walk to Montcliffe?"

"Will you stop and send word to London to have Wilkins, Mrs. Bentham, and Bailey remove to Dove Hill?" Duncan asked. He smiled again at Adelia, seemingly unable to keep his eyes off her for long. "It may be a day or two yet before we are ready to depart."

George gave him a mock bow. "Certainly." He looked again to Davies. "We'll have them send your things as well."

"I should write a personal note," said Davies. When he'd left London, he had thought to return as the same person. Now it seemed that if and when he returned, he would be someone else entirely. And who knew when he might see his fellows again? The abrupt change gnawed at his insides, though he couldn't say why.

"They will understand," said Duncan. "Be happy for you, even."

Davies forced a smile though his throat felt unnaturally tight, his mouth dry.

Seeming to understand Davies' discomfort, Duncan turned to George and changed the subject. "Well, Fitzbert, that leaves you. After you transport Mr. Davies to his new residence, what shall you do? Return to London for the Season? Meet us at Dove Hill?"

"I've been invited to Montcliffe," George said roundly, "by the soon-to-be new lord of the manor."

Duncan blinked surprise, first at George then at Davies. "Really?"

Beside him, Adelia chuckled. "I *told* you they liked each other."

Duncan still appeared nonplussed. "But you have nothing in common. Besides me, that is."

"*De gustibus non est disputandum,*" said Davies with a small smile.

George groaned and rolled his eyes. "Latin! I see I may yet regret my choice."

Davies eyed him, trying to discern how much truth lay behind the words. Why, really, did George Fitzbert want to visit Montcliffe? For the novelty? Just to be able to gloat to his friends? Duncan had spoken often enough of George's love of gossip, something Davies understood well enough—tattle, particularly in London, was currency; a fact as true among servants as gentry. A stay at Montcliffe was unique enough to be worth a great deal on the tongue-wagging market.

George met his gaze, but rather than the expected playfulness and excitement at the prospect of an extended holiday, the amber eyes disclosed caution and... hope? Desire? A shiver ran down Davies' back and his lungs ceased to draw air until he managed to unsnag his gaze from George's.

"You will all be welcome, of course," Davies said, "once I've settled in."

The conversation went on in warm but, Davies thought, not close tones. Despite all they'd gone through and all they'd witnessed, this was an assembly of people soon to disband, and they were keenly aware of it. So much so that they feared tightening their bonds lest it be too painful when the connections unraveled.

As things stood, Richard clearly continued to struggle, his attention wandering from his sister to his brother, brow furrowed as though he were making inward calculations. Now and then he looked at Odette as well, and his slight frown would deepen. *Here*, thought Davies, is *a man whose life has been so changed—his very function in the world made obsolete. He no longer needs to save his sister or care for either of his siblings...* Davies hoped he found a new purpose or created a new family for himself.

"He'll be all right," Edward said, causing Davies to startle. He had not noticed Edward move to stand beside him. The younger Milne brother gave a slight nod in Richard's direction. "We'll take care of him for a change. He deserves the respite."

"I suppose every parent faces the day his children no longer need him," said Davies. "And eventually the parent needs the child to care for him instead."

Edward nodded. "Just as you will your grandfather."

Davies wasn't sure about that, as Lord Montcliffe had seemed fairly capable, whatever the townsfolk and his servants said. "I will have to tell him about Mother," he realized. "That will be a blow."

Odette turned from where she'd been chatting with Adelia.

"That is not necessary. I am happy to visit now and then if need be."

Edward's face lit up. "And me?"

Odette smiled. "Of course. I will require you to help me hold a solid form."

But Davies frowned. "It doesn't seem right to lie."

"Never mind that, Galahad," said George, and at Davies' surprised look, "I didn't live with Henry for twenty-eight years and never learn anything.

"In any case," he continued, "you might be doing the poor old man a service. Telling him the truth could break his heart and kill him on the spot. Unless you're that eager for the title?"

Davies' mouth fell open in consternation. "Of course not! I—"

He stopped short when George laughed. "You're too easy," he said and then sighed. "And in some ways not easy enough."

The room grew awkwardly silent. That, or Davies simply couldn't hear over the blood that rushed through his ears to warm his face. He desperately wanted to scan the faces around him, to read them for signs that the others had inferred the same thing he had from George's words, but he was afraid of what his own expression might give away. So he set the glass of wine he held—where had it come from? he couldn't recall—on the table and said, "I think, if we're to get an early start, I'd best to bed."

"Not too early, I hope," said George. He set his drink down as well. "Though I think I'll go pack so as to be ready."

Davies' heart picked up speed, though he schooled himself and made sure of his proper and polite good-nights as he and George exited the dining room. He found himself unable to look at George as they crossed the entry and made their way upstairs. The sight of their bedroom doors relieved the pressure in him, and he felt nearly able to breathe again until George said, "I don't suppose you'd care to help me undress?"

Davies froze. Swallowing hard, he said without turning, "You seem to forget I'm no longer a valet."

"Oh, I haven't forgotten that at all, *my lord*."

Finally he mustered the courage to look George in the eye. The playfulness was there this time, but something about the set of George's mouth suggested apprehension. Davies understood —this was dangerous. It had to remain deniable, even to the other party, until the interest was clearly returned. Then it became a covert game of hiding it from the rest of the world.

Davies knew. He'd done it before, with Wynn. He wasn't sure he could take another painful parting as that one had been.

And George Fitzbert was such a botheration, as Duncan had often called him. But a charming one. Duncan often admitted that much, too. And Davies suspected gold resided under the surface, if one only scraped off the excess.

Davies had to confess, if only to himself—he *liked* George Fitzbert. A lot. More than was warranted, and certainly more than he ought.

"You do need someone to put your wardrobe to rights," Davies said. "All that claret." He shook his head.

"I can't wear only brown!" George exclaimed.

"I never said you had to," Davies told him. "There are blues and greens that would work with your coloring. The jacket your brother was wearing—"

"Dress like Henry?!"

Davies sighed and made meaningful eye contact. Time to put it on the line. "Do you want my help or don't you?"

George's amber gaze traveled over Davies' face, and Davies knew he was seeking the nuance behind the words. So, *so* dangerous to make a mistake at this juncture. But evidently he found what he wanted, for he smiled. "Yes," he said, "I absolutely do."

"Mother keeps insisting I've outstayed my welcome," said George as he skimmed the letter. He sat in the Montcliffe parlour, nattily dressed in rifle green. Davies insisted the color made his hair and eyes more golden without making his skin tone too yellow. Well, if Davies liked it, that was enough for George.

"Do you want to go back to London?" Davies asked from where he sat at the writing desk, himself busy with correspondence. "So long as you return in time for the wedding..."

"When are they arriving?" George asked.

"End of the week, but the wedding is not for a fortnight yet."

"Good of you to offer them use of the estate. No, I will wait until after to go home, I think," George decided. "Mother and Henry will be coming to the nuptials at any rate. I can go back with them." He paused and eyed the back of Davies' bent head, admiring the curve of his neck. "Will you miss me?"

"Not as much as you'll miss me," said Davies as he signed whatever missive he'd been writing with a flourish.

George rose. "I hate when you're right."

"Which is most of the time." Davies turned in his chair. "Where are you off to?"

"A ride. Oh! Should we invite Percy for dinner tonight?"

"My grandfather *has* grown rather fond of him, I think," Davies said. "Might rally his spirits."

George frowned. He could not deny that Davies had grown close to his grandfather quickly in the six months since installing himself at Montcliffe. But the old man's health was in steady decline. It would be a blow when the inevitable occurred.

But that day the sun shone and all was as well as could be. Duncan and Adelia would soon tie the knot, and George suspected Edward and Odette were not long after. As for Richard, word from Duncan revealed he'd established himself solidly at Dove Hill and all but ran the estate. Just as well, since Duncan never knew what to do with it; his letters signaled a certain amount of relief at having Richard take over.

"It's a wonder they didn't choose Faebourne, though," George mused aloud.

"Not at all," said Davies, picking up as always on George's winding thread of thought. No one, not even Henry, had ever understood him so well. "She'd spent her entire life trapped there. It may be a long time yet before she wants to go back."

A fair point, but George did not feel the need to let Davies know he was right. Again. He turned for the door. "I'm off. Unless you'd care to ride with me?"

Davies smiled and shook his head. It was an ongoing wrangle —George offering to teach Davies to ride, and Davies carefully evading learning.

"One day," George said. "Master of such a place needs to be able to ride."

"One day," Davies agreed. "But not today."

With a swift check that the door was closed and they would not be caught, George crossed the room and gave Davies a quick kiss. Davies blushed but did not look displeased.

"Go on," he said. "I've more letters to write."

George gladly escaped into the fresh autumn air, crisp and cool, the sun no more than a false lure for those seeking warmth. Lucky for him, he was not. He much preferred to ride in the brisk weather.

The stable lads nodded to him; he'd become a fixture at Montcliffe, and if anyone suspected his relationship with Davies, they pointedly looked the other way. Ah, the benefits of being heir to a title (and the lover of one)—few people would cross a one, particularly if they valued their employment. And the staff did seem to be fond of Davies, certainly more so than Nash. Why shouldn't they be? Davies—Viscount Sonnenleigh—was young, handsome, friendly, kind, fair, and by all accounts Lord Montcliffe had become that much easier to manage since having his grandson under his roof. Indeed, suddenly all of Birchmere had nothing but the most charitable words regarding the old man. Lord Montcliffe had gone from "crotchety," "a stickler," and "querulous" to "upstanding," "generous," and "an old dear."

It helped that Davies invited people like Percy Harding to dine now and then. He was slowly rooting himself in Birchmere society. George suspected he would thrive, though already there were pressures for Davies to consider marrying and furthering the Montcliffe line.

A worry for another day. George saddled Thunder and promised Storm a ride on the morrow. "Only one of me," he said. "But we'll get him out here yet, eh?"

Storm snorted and Thunder responded with a snuffle of his own.

"My sentiments exactly," said George. He swung himself into the saddle and set off for town. Maybe he'd stop at the Crown and Cups for the latest gossip. Percy might be there; he could deliver the invitation for dinner.

Or perhaps he'd ride toward Faebourne. He did, now and then, taking the road past the church, but he'd yet to find the house again. Some day, though, when the time was right, George felt sure it would reveal itself once more. When it needed them. Or when they needed it. Whichever came first, if either ever came at all.

ALSO BY M PEPPER LANGLINAIS

Brynnde: A Regency Romance